Th

Sōseki Natsume (1867–1916) is widely considered the foremost novelist of the Meiji period (1868–1914). After graduating from Tokyo Imperial University in 1893, Sōseki taught high school before spending two years in England on a Japanese government scholarship. He returned to lecture in English literature at the university. Numerous nervous disorders forced him to give up teaching in 1908 and he became a full-time writer for the *Asahi* newspaper. In addition to fourteen novels, Sōseki wrote haiku, poems in the Chinese style, academic papers on literary theory, essays, autobiographical sketches and fairy tales.

Sammy I. Tsunematsu is founder and curator of the Sōseki Museum in London, and the translator of several of Sōseki's works. He has also researched and published widely on the Japanese artist Yoshio Markino, who was a contemporary of Sōseki's living in London at the beginning of the twentieth century. Tsunematsu has lived in Surrey, England, for thirty years.

Sōseki Natsume

The Heredity of Taste

Translated by Sammy I. Tsunematsu

With an Introduction by Stephen W. Kohl

TUTTLE PUBLISHING
Boston • Rutland, Vermont • Tokyo

Published by Tuttle Publishing, an imprint of Periplus Editions (HK) Ltd,
with editorial offices at 153 Milk Street, Boston, Massachusetts, 01209 and
130 Joo Seng Road #06-01, Singapore 368357

Originally published as *Shumi no iden*, 1906
English translation © Sammy I. Tsunematsu, 2004
First Tuttle edition, 2004

ISBN 0 8048 3602 7
ISBN 4 8053 0766 8 (for sale in Japan only)

The Translator would like to acknowledge the assistance of
John Edmondson who kindly read through the English version
and made many helpful changes.

Printed in Singapore

Distributed by:

North America, Latin America and Europe
Tuttle Publishing
364 Innovation Drive, North Clarendon, VT 05759-9436.
Tel: (802) 773 8930; Fax: (802) 773 6993;
E-mail: info@tuttlepublishing.com
www.tuttlepublishing.com

Japan
Tuttle Publishing
Yaekari Building, 3F, 5-4-12 Osaki, Shinagawa-ku, Tokyo 141-0032.
Tel: (813) 5437 0171; Fax: (813) 5437 0755;
E-mail: tuttle-sales@gol.com

Asia Pacific
Berkeley Books Pte Ltd
130 Joo Seng Road #06-01, Singapore 368357.
Tel: (65) 6280 1330; Fax: (65) 6280 6290;
E-mail: inquiries@periplus.com.sg
www.periplus.com

This book is dedicated to Yōko Matsuoka McClain,
granddaughter of Sōseki Natsume, who encouraged us
to translate her grandfather's work

OTHER TUTTLE CLASSICS
BY THE SAME AUTHOR

Contents

Sōseki, an Anti-War Writer

In the spring of 2000, to recognize the millennium, the *Asahi Shimbun* newspaper conducted a nation-wide survey asking the Japanese people who they considered was the best Japanese writer of the past one thousand years. Sōseki Natsume was the first choice among readers. Murasaki Shikibu, author of *The Tale of Genji*, was ranked second. Matsuo Bashō, the great haiku poet, ranked sixth. Similarly, there was a great outcry in the fall of 2002 when proposed high school textbooks submitted for approval by the Ministry of Education did not include selections from the *oeuvre* of Sōseki Natsume. Clearly Sōseki is a literary institution in Japan, an author whose work has spoken to generations of Japanese readers, an author who, eighty years after his death, still dominates Japan's literary scene.

More perhaps than any other Japanese writer, the bulk of Sōseki's works have been translated into English, and yet there still remain a host of letters, diaries, poems, and short early works which are unknown outside Japan. These early works are of particular interest because they reveal the extent to which Sōseki was a protean, ever experimental writer, seeking a medium, themes, and methodology that would allow him to express his ideas clearly.

Nearly four decades ago, Professor Edwin McClellan performed a great service when he outlined for English readers the progression of themes in Sōseki's major novels. In this progression, McClellan shows a particular line of philosophical development in Sōseki's work. Today, we have a chance to look at Sōseki's shorter work and see the rich creativity and diversity he brought to his writing.

Shumi no iden, translated here as *The Heredity of Taste*, was written in December 1905 just following the conclusion of the Russo-Japanese War the previous September, and it stands as Sōseki's response to this great and tragic war. This is Sōseki's only work of anti-war literature, and in some ways it marks him as a renegade in Meiji society. The response of the Japanese public to this war was highly ambivalent. On the one hand, the war confirmed Japan's maturity as a modern nation. The proof of this was that she had engaged a major European power in war and had come away the victor. In an age which firmly believed that no non Euro-American people could defeat Europeans in war, Japan had done just that. Admiral Togo had destroyed the Russian naval fleet at Tsushima, and General Nogi had broken General Stoessel's defense of Port Arthur. This victory established Japan's position as the strongest military power in East Asia and guaranteed her a seat as one of the five major victorious nations at the Treaty of Versailles following World War I. In other words, Japan had arrived as a modern world power.

This success, however, had cost Japan dearly both in economic terms and, more significantly, in terms of blood shed by its youth. While patriotism and nationalism were at a fever pitch throughout the nation, there were some who began to question the price Japan had paid for this victory. And when the Treaty of Portsmouth, brokered by President Teddy Roosevelt, left Japan without

$600,000,000 in reparations to recoup the cost of the war, there was a huge outcry in Japan against the government for winning the war with the sacrifice of soldiers, but losing the peace negotiations by caving in to the demands of others. There was rioting in Hibiya Park and martial law was imposed, remaining in effect until the end of November 1905. General Nogi returned from the front on January 14, 1906.

Between these two events, Sōseki wrote this story in which he speaks out against the atrocity of war and the sacrifice of soldiers' lives, but he also protests the degradation of the individual implied by a military uniform and the mindless, squirming mass of advancing soldiers. When he envisions troops struggling up the hill in a serpentine mass, the only thing that makes his friend Kō-san stand out is the fact that he is carrying the regimental flag. Otherwise this golden boy would be indistinguishable from the mass of other soldiers. For Sōseki, it was not only the loss of life that was to be regretted, but also the loss of individuality.

Shumi no iden opens with an impressionistic, dream-like account of the loosing of the dogs of war, emphasizing the violence of the conflict. Waking from this reverie, the narrator finds himself at Shimbashi Station just as the troop trains are returning in triumph from the front. Among the returning soldiers he sees one who is the very image of his friend Kō-san, a sergeant welcomed home by his mother. This leads the narrator to imagine Kō-san's death in the assault on Port Arthur. He has a vision of soldiers swarming up the hill in a tight, squirming mass. Kō-san, by contrast, is a golden boy, far above the common crowd, and yet in this context all that distinguishes him is the regimental flag which he carries. Nevertheless, he falls into the trench and dies like the others. Throughout the rest of the story we have the refrain, *Kō-san wa agatte konai* (Kō-san could not climb out of the ditch). The drum beat repetition of this line throughout the story continues to remind us of the slaughter of the war.

Observing the returning troops and officers at Shimbashi Station, the narrator notes their graying hair and lined faces, the result of the hardship and strain of battle, and he feels sorry for them, but he feels even more sorry for Kō-san who cannot climb out of the ditch and return from the war. And yet, Kō-san who died is by no means the most abject victim of the war. What about his widowed mother who has been left behind with no one to care for her in her old age? The mother wishes she at least had a daughter-in-law, which would have been sadder still—a woman married for a few weeks, then doomed to a lifetime of widowhood. (This story must have had particular resonance forty years later in the aftermath of World War II when many women found themselves in this situation.)

As the troops return home through the victory arch, Sōseki reminds his readers of the many casualties who did not return from the battlefield, and describes the pathos of those they left behind, a mother who says, "I wouldn't care if he had a wooden leg as long as he came home." Thinking of Kō-san who will not be returning home, the narrator decides to visit his grave. Although Kō-san never climbs out of the ditch at Port Arthur, he had sent clippings of his hair and fingernails to be buried in the event he died.

At the cemetery, the narrator encounters a beautiful and mysterious woman and also a ginko tree in the full splendor of its yellow autumn leaves against a clear blue sky. The lavish description of this tree marks a shift in mood from the violence of war to the pathos of love. The tree itself and its description is reminiscent of a similar scene in Sōseki's novel *Kokoro* where the narrator also passes beneath a golden ginko at the entrance to a cemetery. The ginko tree here is described as *bakeichō*, a ghostly or transformed ginko, a tree which marks a liminal space that is the boundary between the world of the living and the world of the dead. In this way, it serves as a nexus between the death of Kō-san and the existence of the mysterious woman. In some sense, it marks the dividing line between love and war. It implies a question. There is love for a beautiful woman, a mother's love for her son, the domestic love of a marriage, and set against these is the sacrifice required to give up all prospect of love and to die in war. To die in war for what? For the nation? Is patriotism worth this level of sacrifice? Sōseki's intent here is not to celebrate the heroism of Kō-san, but to show the folly of war and the magnitude of the sacrifice made by both the living and the dead.

Sōseki was not the only Japanese writer to speak out in opposition to the war. The poet Yosano Akiko wrote a famous poem in which she asked her brother not to sacrifice his life for this cause. The novelist Otsuka Kusuoko, who had close personal ties to Sōseki, also ended up writing in protest to this war.

Sōseki's narrator passes beneath the radiant ginko tree and encounters a beautiful, mysterious woman praying at Kō-san's grave. As she leaves the cemetery, the narrator sees her pause outlined against the ginko tree, its golden leaves, like falling soldiers, swirling down around her. What better image can there be for death than the fallen leaf which can never be reattached to the tree?

The second half of the story centers on finding out the identity of this woman and her relationship with Kō-san. Sōseki famously disliked mystery fiction as a literary genre, and yet here we see him using the techniques of the mystery writer to advance his story. Perhaps we hear an echo of this in the text itself when Sōseki, speaking through his narrator, declares his revulsion for private investigators and yet finds himself behaving like one in his pursuit of the woman's identity.

In search of the woman, the narrator first goes to Kō-san's mother where he sees white chrysanthemums in the garden and learns that they were Kō-san's favorite flower, the same flower the woman had left at the grave. This reinforces the link between Kō-san and the mysterious woman even though the mother insists that her son was not involved with anyone, and that there was no female family member of that age. A perusal of Kō-san's diary reveals that he had erased a passage that speaks of meeting a woman at the post office. At the end of the diary, Kō-san predicts that if he dies in the war, someone will bring white chrysanthemums to his grave. This not only anticipates what actually happens, it also brings together the two main strands of the story, love and war, eros and thanatos.

The second part of the story deals with the matter of love between Kō-san and the woman, but the story line begins to break down at this point. The narrator tells us clearly, "From here on I will abbreviate my story." In this sense, the work might be considered as another of Sōseki's unfinished novels. Although the focus in this second part of the story is on the love between Kō-san and the woman, we are never told how she learned of Kō-san's death or where his grave was located. We never learn why Kō-san felt compelled to erase part of his diary. The abbreviated style that leaves these questions hanging is especially evident in contrast to the earlier scenes at Shimbashi Station which are so long and detailed.

The most important aspect of this second part of the story dealing with love is the way Kō-san is remembered after his death. He lives on in the memory of the woman, he lives on in the memory of his mother, and he lives on in the memory of his friend. But what a poor substitute these memories are for a real and meaningful love relationship. In this sense, what should have been a love story has been shattered by the reality of war. For Kō-san's love for the woman consists only of a single brief encounter and exists only as a dream. For the woman, love which should be lived out in daily life exists only in visits to the grave and in memories.

This story may be added to the list of Sōseki's stories of failed love, yet the poignancy of the failure of these two young people to be together in a loving relationship is an expression of the losses suffered during the war. Instead of telling us how many thousands of young men died at Port Arthur, he shows us the full, tragic implications of a single death and leaves it to us as readers to multiply this tragedy by uncounted thousands. In this context, the repetition of the refrain, "But Kō-san did not climb out of the ditch," is a steady reminder of the magnitude of Japan's sacrifice for this so-called victory.

Finally, we have the matter of Sōseki's notion of the heredity of taste. He was raised in an age when theories of evolution and heredity were first being explored scientifically, a time when the mysteries of human psychology were being probed. In many of his works, he explores the question of what attracts a particular man to a particular woman and vice versa. Certainly in the majority of his writing, Sōseki proves himself to be a connoisseur of the failure of love, but here the question is what attracts people in the first place? The suggestion put forth in this story that the heredity of taste skips one generation and reasserts itself, that Kō-san looks exactly like his grandfather and the woman looks exactly like her grandmother and that they are genetically attracted to each other seems simplistic and naïve. Indeed, it sounds less like a modern concept of heredity and more like an old-fashioned view of Buddhist karma where the things that happen in this life are the result of things we did in previous lives. My own view is that Sōseki was not seriously engaging the question of heredity, but was more interested in writing a polemic against war in general and the way in which the modern state forces the individual to forego his individuality and conform to the needs of the state regardless of the sacrifice involved.

STEPHEN W. KOHL
University of Oregon
June 2004

1

Under the influence of the weather, even the gods lose their reason. "Let's exterminate mankind! Let loose the ravenous dogs!" was the cry that resounded from the heavens to the depths of the Sea of Japan and made it rage in all directions. The cry penetrated as far as Manchuria. As soon as they heard it, the Japanese and Russians responded by creating an immense slaughterhouse in the plains to the north of the Continent of Asia, stretching over more than 400 kilometers. So, under the skies, great hordes of ferocious dogs appeared and sped across the vast expanse. These four-legged bullets tore endlessly through the air, scenting fresh flesh. Delirious in their joy, the gods shouted to the dogs "Drink the blood!" Tongues darted out effortlessly like flames and lit up the dark earth with their brilliance. The sound of blood spurting down the beasts' throats echoed across the plains. Then the gods, walking on the edge of the black clouds, clamored "Devour the flesh!" again and again. "Devour the flesh! Devour the flesh!" The dogs all reared up, barking with one voice. Then, without further delay, they tore limbs to pieces with sinister crunching sounds. Opening their deep jaws from ear to ear, snatching at the trunks of the bodies and tugging at them from all sides, they stripped the skin from the bones. At last, when the gods saw that all the flesh had been devoured, their terrifying voices pierced through the clouds that covered the skies: "When you have done with the flesh, go on to the bones and suck them dry! Now, suck the bones!" Dog's teeth are better suited to gnawing bones than to devouring flesh. Created by demented gods, the creatures are equipped with instruments perfectly adapted to carrying out their insane commands. Their teeth have been especially designed by the divinities for that purpose. Of that there can be no doubt. "Make noise! Make noise!" ordered the gods. The dogs planted their fangs with brute force into the bones. Some bones were shattered so that the beasts could eat the marrow. Others were reduced to tiny pieces and made shapes on the earth that might have been paintings. The bones that the dogs' teeth did not manage to destroy were used to sharpen their fangs....

I was lost in my accustomed reverie. As I reached Shimbashi station,[1] I told myself that such images sent shivers down my spine. Paying attention to what was going on around me, I saw that there was a large crowd on the square in front of the station, although an access path of about four meters[2] leading to a triumphal arch,[3] had been left free. From both sides people pressed forward in a long line, which it seemed impossible to pass through. What was going on then?

---

[1] Shimbashi station was built in Tokyo to serve the first Tokyo–Yokohama railway link, inaugurated in 1872. In 1892, the so-called "Tōkaido" line was opened, connecting Shimbashi to Kobe.

[2] 2 kens. One ken is equivalent to 1.82 meters.

[3] At the end of the Russo-Japanese War, an enormous triumphal arch was built in front of Shimbashi station to welcome soldiers returning from the battlefields.

Among the crowd I noticed a suspicious-looking man wearing a silk hat on the back on his head, his ears fortunately preventing his headdress from falling off. Another individual was wearing traditional trousers, which seemed too tight or uncomfortable for him, because he was continually gazing at his silk twill outfit as if it belonged to someone else. A third fellow afforded a very singular spectacle. He was dressed in a frock coat, that I freely acknowledge, but he had put on white canvas shoes and gloves, which he made no attempt to conceal and which in fact he was displaying to all and sundry. A score of people brandished conveniently sized banners. The majority of these bore inscriptions in white characters on a mauve background, but on others someone had prettily emblazoned ebony inscriptions on white fabric. To find out why all these people were assembled there, I started to read the banners and was struck by the one nearest to me, which proclaimed, "The volunteers of the Renjaku[4] district celebrate the triumphal return of Mr Kimura Rokunosuke." I understood then for the first time that an enthusiastic welcome was being organized in honor of somebody; and even the gentlemen I had just seen, decked out in the strange accouterments, acquired a certain distinction in my eyes. Moreover, I quickly began to regret having imagined that war had been provoked by gods who had descended into madness and that soldiers were going to the battlefield to be devoured by dogs. In fact, I was going to the station because I had an appointment to meet

---

[4] A district in Tokyo, situated in the old district of Kanda, today Chiyoda district. It is a major shopping area.

someone. With this crowd amassed all about me, I realized that to get there I would have to walk on my own along the path that split the impenetrable throng. Surely no one here was capable of fathoming those poetic visions that had been in my mind a moment before. Even under normal circumstances I am uncomfortable about walking alone in the road, attracting glances and feeling people's eyes concentrated on my little self. But if they knew that I had imagined their loved ones as leftover dog food, it was safe to assume they would be annoyed. With such thoughts in my mind, I had to fight against unease and reluctance beneath my air of nonchalance as I forged a path to the stone steps of the station.

Once I had reached the building, the next problem was to get inside it. Given the number of people who had turned up to welcome the combatants, it was no easy task to get to the appointed place, and when I did finally arrive at the first-class waiting room I found that the person I had arranged to meet there had not yet come. Near the fireplace, an officer in a red cap was talking enthusiastically, his sword clicking continuously. Next to him were two silk hats, side by side. Above one of them there was a widening ring of cigar smoke. In a corner at the other end of the room, a woman was talking to a fine looking lady of about fifty years of age, whispering so quietly that their conversation could not have been overheard by someone sitting next to them. A man in a traditional "haori" cotton[5] jacket, with his cap sideways on his head, went up to the two ladies and told them that they could not buy platform

---

[5] *Tōzan*, a striped cotton fabric used to make "haori" or kimonos.

tickets because the area beyond the ticket gate was already full of people. He must have been their servant. People in the crowd who had grown tired of waiting were gathered around tables in the center of the room, leafing through newspapers and magazines and rolling them up to kill time. Very few were reading seriously. The expression "leafing through" describes what they were doing perfectly, I think.

The man I was meeting still had not arrived so, bored with waiting, I decided to take a short walk outside. Just then, however, a bearded man walked into the room and said as he passed in front of me, "There is not much longer to wait—the train is expected to arrive at 14.45."

I looked at my watch and saw that it was half past two. So in just quarter of an hour's time, I would be able to see the triumphal return of the soldiers. With apologies for the diversion, I must tell you in passing that people like me, who spend most of their time in libraries, do not generally have the opportunity to wait at Shimbashi station to welcome home combatants. Considering that it would be a good thing to do, I decided to go and watch. As I left the waiting room, I noticed that the people in the station enclosure had formed into queues, as they had done in the road, and that some Westerners who had come to watch the ceremony were now mingling with the crowd. As even Westerners were participating I, a subject of the Emperor, must surely be there to welcome home the soldiers. Telling myself that I really had to go and shout "Banzai!" I slipped into the crowd and joined the queue.

"Have you come here to welcome home a relation too? I was really frightened of being late and came here without any lunch. I've been waiting for two hours."

However hungry this person appeared, he seemed to be in good shape. At that moment, a lady of about thirty arrived and asked a little anxiously, "Will the soldiers who have returned in glory to the Mother Country all pass through here?" The earnest manner in which she spoke to us communicated her deep anxiety that she might miss someone who was dear to her.

The man with the complaining stomach answered reassuredly, "Yes, they will all pass through here, without exception! So you will surely have to stand here for another two to three hours." He spoke with great confidence, but did not go so far as to add that she would have to wait with an empty stomach.

A French novelist has compared the whistle of a train to an asthmatic whale. Just as I was remembering this very appropriate description, the train twisted into the station like a snake and vomited out five hundred hearty-looking people on to the platform.

Someone stretched out his neck and shouted, "The train has arrived, hasn't it?"

"What's the matter?" asked our hungry colleague, "We're all right if we stay here. No problem!" And maintaining his imperturbable calm he showed no intention of moving. To listen to this man, it seemed that it didn't matter whether the train arrived or not. He was phlegmatic in spite of his hunger pangs.

Shortly afterwards, the cry of "Banzai!" erupted on the platform one or two hundred meters in front of us. The shout passed in a wave from one person to another until it came to me.

"What's the matter? No problem, n...."

The people lined up on either side of me shouted in

unison a "Banzai!" that muffled the rest of this utterance from our starving friend. The shouting was still going on when a general, giving a military salute, passed in front of me. He was a short man, with a tanned face and sporting a pepper-and-salt beard. The people at my side, seeing that the general was leaving, once again shouted "Banzai!" Now, it may seem strange but I had never once in all my life shouted "Banzai!" It was not that, as far as I can remember, anyone ever told me not to. Nor was it because I disapproved of it—obviously there is nothing objectionable about it. But, impeded by this lack of experience, now that I was on the point of crying out "Banzai!," no sound came out of my mouth, as if I had a pebble stuck in my windpipe. Whatever I did, the "Banzai!" remained stuck in my throat, noiseless; however hard I tried, I could make no sound. Nevertheless, I had determined some time in advance that a sound would indeed come out of my mouth. In fact, I had been telling myself as I waited that it would be best if the opportunity would present itself as soon as possible. I was not the man next to me; but I found it reassuring to insist to myself that there was no problem. As soon as the asthmatic whale had bellowed, I had held myself in readiness for the moment that was to come, and when the people surrounding me had shouted so loudly, I tried instantly to join in. In fact, it is strictly true that the "Banzai!" had started to rise from the depths of my throat, but the general had passed at the very moment it reached my mouth. And then I saw his tanned face and his pepper-and-salt beard and my "Banzai!" was stillborn. Why?

How could I know why? To understand something and identify the precise reason for it, we need to reflect calmly on the event after it has happened. It is only by going over the facts and analyzing them that we can arrive at an understanding of them. If I had known why the cry would be strangled in my throat, well, I would have taken steps at the outset and made sure that my "Banzai!" did not stick in my gullet. If it were possible to address human actions in that way, how peaceful human history would be! It must be said that my "Banzai!" had been blocked by something transcendent, beyond the scope of my right of intervention. At the same time as the "Banzai!" was blocked, spasms difficult to describe shook my breast and two tears rolled down my face.

Perhaps the general had a swarthy face from birth? But most people who have endured the winds from the Liatong[6] peninsula, or experienced the Moukden[7] rains or been burned by the sun at Shu he,[8] come back darker skinned than they left. Someone whose complexion is naturally pale will become browner. It is the same with a beard. A few white strands will probably appear in a black beard once its owner has left for the front. Those of us who were looking at the general for the first time, had no way of drawing a comparison between what he had been before and what he was now. Presumably his wife and daughters, who had anxiously counted the days and nights, would be surprised by what they saw. War, when it

---

[6] The most northerly area of China.

[7] Capital of the Chinese province of Liaoning. Shenyang (Chen-Yang), formerly Moukden, is situated on the Hun He, in the heart of the plain of Liaohe.

[8] Shu he is 15 kilometers to the south of Moukden.

does not kill people, ages them. The general was extremely thin, but perhaps his thinness was attributable to the cares he had endured. The only aspect of his physique that could not have changed from what it was before he left for the front was his height. People like me who live with their noses in books are like hermits, withdrawn from the world, and we know nothing of what is happening beyond our places of work. This is not to say that I do not ordinarily read newspapers or express my views on the war poetically. However, the imagination is limited to fantasy, and the newspapers, however intently we read them every day from front to back, end up as waste paper. Thus, when there is a war, we do not genuinely feel as if it is really taking place. For a carefree person like me, fortuitously engulfed in the crowd that invaded the station, what most struck me was that face burned by the sun and that beard tinted with frost. I have never seen war with my own eyes, but when the consequences had furtively passed in front of me, or, more precisely, a fragment of the consequences, and moreover a living fragment, under the influence of that fragment I could see very clearly in my mind's eye the post-combat scenes on the plain of Manchuria.

Furthermore, all around that little fragment, which we can consider as an image of the war, were the cheers of the people shouting "Banzai!" This was nothing more than the echo of the war cries that had resounded on the Manchurian battlefield. The meaning of "Banzai!," if we take the literal interpretation of the Chinese characters that comprise it, is "May you live for a thousand years!" When a war cry sounds, on the other hand, its form and meaning differ singularly. The war cry is a short and simple "Aaah!" Unlike "Banzai!," it has no particular meaning, but just because it has no meaning does not prevent it from having an extreme and deep significance. There are different kinds of human voices. Some are piercing, others harsh, some clear, some deep. The linguistic structures and inflections they express are equally varied. For 23 hours 50 minutes of every 24 hours people use words that have a precise meaning. Whatever "domain," whatever field of knowledge or activity, whether it is clothing or food, negotiations or deals, greetings or trivial gossip, everything can be expressed vocally. Ultimately, it could even be argued that a domain does not exist if nobody is talking about it. But people do not usually utter sounds that make no sense and do not refer to a particular domain. In purely economic or utilitarian terms, however often we may utter a particular sound, we will be wasting our vocal energy if it has no recognizable meaning. Only in extreme situations are we forced to try to make ourselves understood through apparently meaningless sounds which needlessly assault the eardrums of innocent people. The war cry is a vocal distillation of the emotions of someone in a critical situation or threatened by great danger. It is a natural cry of the deepest sincerity which rises straight up from the depths of the diaphragm when a man, his whole body trembling, balances dangerously on a tensed metal wire, hovering between life and death, between this free world and hell. When someone yells "Help!" the sincerity of his cry is clearly expressed in the word. The howl "I am going to kill you!" is clearly not without credibility, but precisely because the words have a meaning, the degree of certainty is reduced. As long as we retain sufficient discernment to use words that make sense, it cannot be said that we are uttering truth straight from the heart, unalloyed with anything else. Moreover, there is not the slightest crumb of humanity in a war cry. The war cry is "Aaah!" In a war cry there is no sarcasm or common sense. It contains no good or evil. It is as devoid of falsehood as it is of any attempt to manipulate. It is, from beginning to end, only "Aaah!" The emotion that it crystalizes, explodes and sends out shock waves in all directions; that is what causes this "Aaah!" to resonate. It has not that sense of sinister augury conveyed in expressions like "Banzai!," "Help!," or even "I am going to kill you!" In other words, "Aaah!" is mind; "Aaah!" is soul; "Aaah!" is humanity; "Aaah!" is truth. And I think that it is only when we are able to hear this truth expressed simultaneously by tens, hundreds, thousands and tens of thousands of people that we can appreciate the supreme, unfathomable and infinite dimension of it. The fresh tears that rolled down my face when I saw the general were perhaps a reaction to this sense of a supreme truth.

After the general, two or three officers passed in front of us, sporting the new tan-colored uniform. They had apparently come to meet the general, judging from their expressions, which were very different from his. I have known from childhood, because I have heard it so often, that saying of Mencius,[9] "the dwelling changes the attitude of the mind," but now, seeing how much the faces of those returning from the war differed from the faces of those who had stayed in the city, I felt I understood it

---

[9] The Chinese thinker Mencius (370–290). Mencius (Mengzi, "Master Meng") lived in the second half of the fourth century. Like Confucius and Mozi, he came from the Lu country. A philosopher and writer, he renewed the doctrine of Confucius.

more acutely than ever before. I wanted to see the general's face once again, for good or evil, and I stood on the tips of my toes—but in vain! I could see only a crowd of several tens of thousands of people, gathered outside the station and shouting war cries so loudly that I thought they would shatter the station windows. The crowd all around me finally broke the ranks it had formed and headed in a mass towards the main entrance. It seemed to me that the people shared my desire to see the general again. I, too, pushed by the black wave, was carried three or four meters in the direction of the stone steps, but when I got to this point I could not go any further. At such times—when, for example, I am leaving a Yose[10] show by a narrow doorway, or have to take a tram to meet someone, or must buy a railway ticket at a busy station, in fact whenever I have to compete with other people in a crowd—at such times my nature counts against me and I always end up at a disadvantage. More often than not on such occasions I end up last, well behind everyone else. The present case was no exception—I was very easily passed by the other people. It was not just that I allowed myself to be overtaken in a normal way: I was effectively relegated to the back and that was really depressing! If, at a funeral reception, I don't reach out assertively and don't manage to get my rice with red beans[11] cooked, it doesn't

---

[10] A hall where the working classes go to hear storytellers, lectures, concerts or conjurers, and attend comic shows.

[11] *Sekihan*, rice cooked with sugared red beans. This dish is very popular and is traditionally served on special family occasions, such as the feast of Majority (15 January), admission to primary school or university, success in an examination, a wedding breakfast or, a more intimate event, the onset of puberty of the young lady of the house.

matter to me. However, to fail to contemplate a representative of the vitality and energy that determine the destiny of the Japanese empire, that was really a shame! One way or another, I was determined to see the general. Shouts of "Banzai!" resounded everywhere; they filled the air and assaulted my eardrums with the power of great waves breaking on the rocks. The noise became unbearable. I had to see what was going on. Suddenly, I had an idea. The previous spring, I was making my way along a street in the Azabu[12] district when I heard laughter coming from a large house surrounded by a high adobe wall. It sounded as if a lot of people in there were having a good time. Was it because my stomach was giving me trouble that day that I wanted to have a look and find out what was going behind the wall? Yes, I am sure that this sudden desire originated from the state of my stomach. If it had not been for my stomach, such a stupid notion would certainly not have entered my head. But whatever the reason, when you want to see something, you want to see it. And that wish will be as steadfast or as transient as the reason behind it. Anyway, as I have just said, people were laughing on the other side of the wall, and, in the absence of any hole in the wall, I could see no way of satisfying my desire to know what was going on. When circumstances make it seem impossible for us to see what we want to see, the desire just gets stronger. Silly though it may seem, I was firmly resolved not to go on before I had seen inside. However, to go into a house uninvited would be to act like a thief. On the other hand, I was even more perturbed at

---

[12] A district of Tokyo, comprising what are now the central and western parts of the district of Minato-ku.

the thought of having to ask permission to go in. It was disagreeable to reflect that my curiosity to see what was going on would either cause annoyance to the people living there or damage my reputation. I could think of no good stratagem to achieve my aim, other than surveying the premises from the top of a nearby hill or from a hot-air balloon. But neither of these methods seemed very practical under the prevailing circumstances. Well! The only way to solve the problem was to fall back on my own resources. I would resort to the magical technique of the high jump that I had practiced in high school. I would jump up and try to see over the wall: this seemed to me an ingenious plan. Luckily, there was no one else in the street, and anyway, if there had been someone, they would have had no reason to complain. No sooner said than done—I leaped into the air with all the power my legs could bestow. My training produced a remarkable effect. Not only my neck, but my shoulders appeared above the wall, as I had expected. I stared with all my concentration to make sure I didn't miss this great opportunity to satisfy my curiosity. "There, that's certainly where it's coming from!" I said to myself as I saw in a flash four women playing tennis. As if someone had told them to expect me, they all greeted my leap into the air with a loud burst of laughter. With an exclamation of surprise I fell back heavily on to the ground I had just departed from.

Anyone reading this story will find it comical. I myself, the hero of the adventure, think it quite ludicrous, and have not told it to anybody until today. I find myself comical. But whether something is comical or serious depends on the person and circumstances concerned: a leap into the air is intrinsically funny. It is I, jumping up to look at four women playing tennis, who make things funny. Romeo leaping high in the air to see Juliet produces no comical effect. If we agree that the situation in which Romeo finds himself is not comic, I can take the debate one step further. There is nothing comical in the action of jumping up in the air to see a distinguished and glorious man, a general returning in triumph to his homeland. Is the leap comical in a case such as that? Even it were, it would be all the same to me: what I want to see, I want to see, whatever people might think. So I prepared to leap up into the air. Telling myself that it was a good idea and that there was no other way, as in the earlier case, I finally decided to try it. First, I took off my hat and gripped it under my arm, because on the previous occasion, due to lack of experience, gravity had brought me abruptly back to earth and my new felt hat accordingly rose from my head, without my greeting anyone, and rolled to the other side of the street two meters ahead of me. I still remember the sardonic laughter of the rickshaw puller who was passing by at the time without a passenger and who stopped to pick up my hat and return it to me. That would not happen this time. I examined the position of the hat closely to reassure myself that all was in order and, feeling as if the ends of my toenails were pressing into the pavement, I adjusted my position and leaned forward. Since I had fortunately been pushed to the back by the crowd, there was no one nearby I could upset. The shouts of joy that had died down for a moment burst out again on all sides, just as at high tide the waves break over and over again on the rocks. Telling myself "Now's the time!" I leaped up into the air with such force that my legs felt as if they were going to plunge into my thorax.

There he was! There he was, sitting in a landau with the hood down—it had just passed by the triumphal arch. As before, with cries mingling together all around him in the hubbub and chaos, his tanned face stood out in the crowd like a point of light emanating from the past. I saw a horse among the guard of honor coming to meet him, rear up on his hind legs, terrified by the shouts of "Banzai!," and begin to swerve from his route in the direction of the crowd. I saw the violet banner that floated above the general's carriage leaning over precariously. At a second-floor window of an inn at the corner of a road leading out on to the Shimbashi highway, I saw a woman in a purple kimono with silver reflections waving a white handkerchief.

Before I could really grasp what I was seeing, my feet touched the ground of the station again. It all happened in the blink of an eye. Just as our vision always seems to be obscured after a flash of lightning has shed a brilliant light on everything around us, I fell back to the ground and was plunged into a deep reverie.

When the general had gone, any discipline that had restrained the crowd disappeared, and what order had prevailed till then was lost. The mass of humanity that had formed the queue melted away and the black mountain that had seemed rock solid started to move. The crowd began to thin out in places that had been filled to the brim. People were hurrying to leave. At the same time, the soldiers who had got off the train with the general were beginning to arrive on foot from the station in small detachments. The color of their uniforms had faded. Instead of gaiters, they had rolled folded yellow woolen cloths around their legs, from ankle to knee. Every one of them had allowed his beard to grow abundantly and their faces could not be more tanned. Soldiers are part of war, and they are also the pure product of "the soul of Japan."[13] Businessmen are useless to the nation, as are journalists and geishas—and, of course, people like me who spend their lives with their noses in books! Only these living monuments, who have let their beards grow long and who might almost be mistaken for tramps, are absolutely necessary. Not only do they represent the spirit of Japan, but, more than that, they embody a spirit common to all humanity. The spirit of humanity is not calculated on abacuses, nor is it obtained by entering into perfect harmony with the shamisen. It cannot be expressed in a short essay nor found in a large encyclopedia. But this spirit of Japan shines like a faint light in the tanned faces of these grubby and wretched soldiers. When Buddha came down from the mountain, he was not wearing make-up or gold rings; his clothes looked like rags from a refuse tip, sewn together. There were not enough of them to cover his body or protect it from the north wind as it blew the rags from his chest so that you could count his ribs. If Buddha is venerated, why shouldn't we honor soldiers? During the war that came with the Mongol[14] invasion, the Shogun

---

[13] *Yamato damashii*, literally the soul of the Yamato country, an idea forming the basis of the *Kokutai*. This word appeared in the founding texts of the Empire in the Meiji era.

[14] *Genkō*. The Hōjō had to face the Mongol invasion, a hitherto unknown peril. Kublai Khan, in effect, became Master of China and Korea. He heard of the riches of Japan and as early as 1268 tried to exact a tribute.

Tokimune[15] granted an audience to the revered Buddhist Kokushi. All Kokushi did was exclaim: "Exercise your authority and advance with authority!" I doubt that these filthy soldiers would be the subject of such a passionate injunction. The Zen precept contained in the order to advance with authority was fitting for Tokimune and has always been expressed in the rules of military combat. It envisages beings who, imbued with greatness, return to their homes driven by a noble spirit and having complied with the injunction to rush forward with authority. If we attach no value or do not respect the mental discipline that urges these men to the limits of their endurance, that drives them to advance, there is nothing in this universe, in the heavens or the earth below, that deserves the least respect. Ah, the tanned faces! Some among them were so dark that it was hard to believe they were really Japanese. And those beards that had never been cut! They looked as if they had been put through a mangle and then worked on with a sweeping brush. That strength of mind shows itself reservedly at first, as if something were obstructing it. Then, like heated water, it bubbles up and boils over.

Every time a detachment appeared, the crowd shouted "Banzai!" On hearing this, some of the combatants' tanned faces lit up with a smile and they passed before us looking happy. Others, their eyes fixed before them, walked on with a heavy tread. In some faces we read defiance in the face of such a welcome. The soldiers posing proudly

---

[15] Hojō Tokimune (1251–84), 8th regent (*shikken*) of the Hojō house who assumed the hereditary responsibility for leading the military government of Kamakura. In 1264, Tokimune was appointed second and heir presumptive to the governor.

under the welcoming standards watched their comrades arriving from afar. One soldier who had just got to the bottom of the steps felt so comforted by all these people who had come to welcome him that he forgot to salute them and quite unexpectedly shook hands with everyone without the least reserve. He must have been thinking of the custom at the Manchuria front.

Among the soldiers was one who is the origin of this story. He was aged twenty-eight or twenty-nine. Like all the rest of his honorable comrades, he had a tanned face. Following their example, he had grown his beard, probably since the previous year. But in the lines of his face, fine and elegant, he was not like the rest of the troops. Moreover, he was so like my dead friend Kō-san[16] that they might have been brothers. In truth, when this man came down the steps I was so taken aback that I nearly threw myself forward to meet him. But Kō-san was not an NCO: he was a volunteer, an infantry lieutenant. He was also in the good care of the temple of Hakusan.[17] And so, however much I might want to believe that he was Kō-san, I knew that it was impossible. Human nature is strange. Of course, it would been wonderful if this sergeant had died on the field of honor at Port Arthur instead and in place of Kō-san, who would then have come back home, in place of the sergeant, safe and sound. I thought to myself too how happy this would have made his mother. Giving

---

[16] The name of the hero of the story. "Ko" means a vast space, abundance, vigor and also generosity.

[17] A locality in the district of Koishikawa (today Bunkyo-ku). But what is surprising is that there is no temple in the locality. The one the author names as Jakkō-in at Komagome is invented.

free rein to my thoughts, since I was not at all worried that they would be discovered, I stared at this sergeant. He seemed to think that something was amiss and looked persistently all about him. He gave no sign of wanting to leave the station to stride off towardss Shimbashi, as the others were doing. I told myself that he was looking for something, that possibly he was not from Tokyo, that he was unfamiliar with the district and wanted someone to help him out. I watched him closely without taking my eyes off him, and suddenly a woman of about sixty rushed towards him and clung to his sleeve. I wondered how she could have made her way through all that crowd to get there. The man was of average weight but clearly taller than the others, by about five centimeters. By contrast, the woman was shorter than average and was also slightly stooped with age. It was impossible therefore to tell for sure whether she had thrown her arms around his neck or whether she had hugged him. Thinking of a Sino-Japanese term that I have in my mind, I am sure that what I saw is most accurately described by the expression "hanging around his neck." At that moment, the sergeant looked down at the old woman as if he had found something he had lost. The woman lifted her eyes up to the sergeant with the expression of a mother who had at last found her lost child. Shortly afterwards, the sergeant and his mother set off. The mother still hung on to her son. The onlookers around them clapped and cried "Banzai! Banzai!" but the old lady seemed to pay no attention to the shouts and cheers. She allowed herself be drawn on by her son and was content to hang on to his arm and raise her eyes to his face. The sliding along the ground of her rice straw[18] sandals and the footsteps of the soldier's hobnail boots blended together as they went off, swaying and winding in the direction of Shimbashi. Remembering Kō-san, I looked after the two figures in their sandals and heavy boots.

---

[18] *Zōri*, straw sandals.

2

A h Kō-san! Kō-san died at Port Arthur in November last year. The story is that on 26 November a violent wind arose. The assault on the Sung Shu-shan[19] fortress took place as expected, with the great gusts of that autumnal north wind apparently striving to chase the black sun into the sea. It was one o'clock in the afternoon. To cover the attack, our guns began to pound the left flank of the enemy positions, producing a cloud of dust fifteen meters high. This was the signal for the assault and the soldiers, in their hundreds (it was impossible to estimate their number), immediately left the trenches and began the attack. Like ants when someone has kicked their nest, the men swarmed up the mountain in front of the fortress. From a distance it was impossible to see how anyone could find their way up the slope because of the network of barbed wire that the enemy had laid along it. However, each soldier managed to work his way through it, with the help of a ladder which he carried on his shoulder or a bag of earth. The sappers, by cutting through the wire,

---

[19] Situated to the north of Port Arthur. The Japanese army, digging tunnels, besieged the stronghold after the bitter combat of December 31, 1904. The story of the operation features in Sōseki's *Travels in Manchuria and in Korea* (1910; English translation 2000).

had opened up a path less than four meters wide, and now the rapidly advancing élite solders were quarreling over it as they strove to make their way along it, pushed on by the masses behind them. From where I stood, it looked as if a black river was flowing straight up the hill and cutting it in two. The enemy shells crashed mercilessly in the midst of this black flowing mass and produced so much smoke that everything was obscured. The north wind tore the smoke into tatters, made it fly away in all directions and dragged it towards the distant sky. When the smoke cleared, I saw that the black creatures were continuing to swarm and squirm, just as before. Kō-san was among them. In the days when we sat talking around a brazier, Kō-san made a strong impression. He was an elegant man, with a brown complexion and a thick beard. When he began to tell an amusing story, he would grab everyone's attention. We would forget today. We would forget tomorrow. Under the spell of Kō-san, we would even forget ourselves: everything would disappear except Kō-san, who was unique. So Kō-san had a strong personality and I had always thought that, wherever he went, everything would go well for him and that he was made to attract the attention of others. In light of this I am not comfortable about using a vulgar verb like "squirm" to describe Kō-san— but, just then, he was squirming as I watched. He was squirming like an ant on the end of a pickaxe that someone has used to dig up an anthill and destroy it. He was squirming like a baby spider trapped by the water from a long ladle. In such a situation, even personalities as strong as Kō-san's have no chance of surviving. Facing the great mountain, the vast sky, and the autumnal north wind which swept across the immense expanse, faced with the smoke that enveloped everything with its thick mantle, facing the shells that spat out of the guns and roared through the air, even the greatness of men like Kō-san was no longer apparent. He became as insignificant as a grain of soya in a straw bag. Ah, Kō-san! Where are you? What are you doing? How good it would be if you could become once again the man you were and amaze the Russkies!

Every time a shell landed those black creatures suddenly dispersed and then regrouped. As I wondered whether they had all evaporated into the air, I would see them begin to move again through the encircling smoke. Sometimes the mass began to move again like a snake crawling over a wall, each part of its body along its whole length wriggling frantically until it managed to get its complete body moving forward smoothly and then it would climb again, little by little. And now they had reached the enemy stronghold already! Kō-san had to go in first! Through the gaps in the curling smoke we could see something at the head of the black snake that bent in the wind and that looked like a flag. Was it the power of the wind or human action that made the bearer fall back down the mountain? Whatever it was, he fell sharply, but I thought that I would see him stand upright again in front of me. As I became dismayed and wondered whether he had fallen for good, he rose again and reached towards the sky. Then, he went back to his position and leaned forward. It is Kō-san! It is Kō-san! It could not be anyone else. If several people started to argue bitterly with one another and one single person could attract their attention in the middle of the din, that person could only be Kō-san. You consider your wife a great beauty who surpasses all other women. If your ravishing wife goes to a party and no one picks her out as superior to the other women present, you will be discontented. In your house, you treat your son as a young lord—he has everything he wants and is the sole young master of all he surveys. But once the young master puts on a school uniform and takes the road to school, you will no doubt be dissatisfied when he sits next to the son of the haberdasher who lives opposite you and, to cap it all, you find there is not the slightest difference between the two. It was exactly the same with my friend Kō-san. Wherever he went, if he did not behave as Kō-san usually behaved, I would be dissatisfied. If, like a sweet potato crushed in a mortar, he were trapped in the mêlée and confusion, this would not be at all like the real Kō-san. So if there was someone doing something distinctive, it didn't matter what—waving the flag, flourishing his sword above his head—to attract the attention of others in this disorder and confusion, I wanted it to be Kō-san. And it was not just that I wanted it. I willed with all my power that the person acting that way would be him. Even if I was wrong, it would have been impossible for me to imagine such an unworthy thing as a mediocre Kō-san who did not stand out from the mass. This being the case, the standard-bearer had to be Kō-san.

As the black mass had now arrived at the foot of the stronghold, I told myself that it would soon reach the surrounding wall and start to climb it. Suddenly, part of the snake's head was severed and disappeared from sight. It was strange! We didn't see them hit by shells and killed. Nor did we see them throw themselves to the ground to avoid sniper fire. What had happened? At this point, what was left of the snake's head disappeared abruptly in its turn. I looked on, mystified. As more soldiers started out from the foot of the mountain and climbed to the fortress, pushed on by others behind them, they too disappeared suddenly, as soon as they had arrived at a particular point. And as yet no one had started to climb the wall of the fortress. There was a ditch there, separating the enemy stronghold and our soldiers. Unless it was crossed no one could approach the enemy. This is why the soldiers had climbed courageously to the summit along the path that had been opened through the barbed wire, and they had finally reached the edge of this ditch. Then, not one or two men but the whole detachment had jumped into the deep pit. I understood now that they had brought ladders to scale the wall and bags of earth to empty into the ditch. I didn't know how much the ditch had been filled in, but following a strategy worked out in advance the solders had jumped into it at the nearest point and had all disappeared from view. They were still jumping in and disappearing when Kō-san's turn arrived. Here is Kō-san at last! Go on, my lad! You must hold the standard firmly! The flag that stood out against the sky looked as if it might be torn to pieces by the gusting wind. Suddenly, the pole bent forward sharply, and I thought it had broken. At that precise moment, Kō-san disappeared. Look, he has finally jumped! Then five or six shells launched from the fortress of Erh Lung-Shan[20] all exploded at once on the mountainside, tearing at the violent wind whose complaints filled the air with such tremendous noise that we thought the mountain itself had been decapitated, cut off from its

---

[20] Stronghold of Ehr Lung-Shan situated in a district north of Port Arthur. It was besieged by the Japanese army on 29 December 1904.

foundations in the wind. The cloud of dust from the explosion invaded everywhere that the early winter sun illuminated, and covered, as if it had sealed it up, the countryside all around. It was as if it had been painted out in front of my eyes. I didn't know what could have happened to Kō-san. I was extremely worried. I thought he must have been right in the middle of this whirling smoke and I strained with all my might to see what was happening. It was like looking at a distant rainstorm: the heavy dust cloud that enveloped everything remained dense, despite the violent wind which I would have thought would have driven it away and solved the problem. But it remained, regardless of my impatience. Two minutes passed. It was useless for me to rub my eyes over and over again: nothing helped, and it was as if I had been struck blind. However, I was convinced that I would be able to make out what was happening if the smoke dispersed. And what I would see would be Kō-san's flag, on the other side of the ditch, which would flutter in the sun and reflect the light. I was in no doubt of that, nor that he would have climbed up high on the other side of the ditch and that I would see the Japanese flag on the parapet of the fort, floating high in the air and flapping in the wind. With Kō-san on the scene, you knew that something like that would happen, regardless of what the other people involved were doing. It would have been so much better if all the smoke had lifted rapidly. Why didn't it disappear?

At last! We could just make out a corner of the left wing of the enemy fortress. Then the solid stone wall also began to reappear. But we saw no sign of any human being. Alas! That was strange! The flag should already have been on its way, moving forward. What was happening? By then Kō-san should have been halfway up the mound of earth below the wall of the stronghold. The smoke cleared gradually as if someone were sweeping it away from top to bottom with a broom. I could not see Kō-san anywhere. This looked bad! The other members of his detachment that I had seen squirming like river snails had disappeared too. That made things look even worse. I couldn't understand why they didn't come out of their hiding places. Five seconds passed. I wondered whether they were ready yet to come out. Ten seconds passed, then twenty, then thirty seconds, and all in vain—no soldier came out of the ditch to continue the advance. And this did not change. Those who had jumped into that trench had not done so to cross it and climb up the other side: they had jumped in to die there. As soon as their feet had touched the bottom of the pit, machine guns, which had been trained on the trench awaiting their arrival, opened fire on them. The guns sounded like sticks being dragged along a bamboo fence—"rat, tat, tat, tat …"—and they transferred the soldiers from life to death in the blink of an eye. It was not possible for the dead to crawl up out of the trench. It was absurd to expect people who were lying in a deep ditch, piled one on top of the other like pieces of fat radish preserved in brine, to follow the simple order that had been given to them and climb up the other side. The men lying there would certainly have wanted to be able to climb: it was because they had wanted to reach the other side that they had dived into the ditch like that. But however much a man wanted to climb out, if his limbs would not move, it could not be done. If his eyes were growing dim, he could not climb. If he had a hole in his chest, he could not climb. If his blood did not circulate, if his brain was crushed, if his shoulder was wrenched out, if his body had stiffened like a walking stick, he could not climb. It was not just when the smoke from the guns of the Ehr Lung-Shan fortress had cleared that he could no longer climb. It would be so too when the cold sun of Port Arthur had sunk into the sea and frost again covered the surrounding mountains that it would be impossible to climb. Even when General Stessel[21] had surrendered and all twenty forts were returned to Japanese hands, it would be impossible to climb. Even when the Russo–Japanese peace treaty[22] had been signed, and General Nogi[23] had made a triumphal return to our country, and was fêted as was fitting for that happy event, it would be impossible to climb from the ditch. Even if, during the thirty-six thousand days that would make up the century to come, we moved heaven and earth to meet them, it would be impossible for those men to climb up out of the trench. They met their fate when they jumped into that trench. And it

---

[21] Anatoli Mikhailovitch Stessel (1848–1915) was the commander-in-chief of the Russian garrison of Port Arthur. Besieged by the Japanese armies under the command of General Nogi, after waging a defensive war for several months he was forced to surrender. For this he appeared before the Russian war council and was condemned to death. But his sentence was later commuted and he was eventually freed.

[22] The peace treaty of Portsmouth was signed on September 5, 1905 under the arbitration of the United States by Komura Jutarō for Japan and Witte for Russia.

[23] General Nogi Maresuke (1849–1912), victor of Port Arthur and of the battle of Moukden, figures emblematically as the soul of Japan "Yamato damashii," previously quoted by the author. He ended his own life as well as that of his wife when the Emperor Meiji died, so as not to survive him.

was Kō-san's fate too. After squirming about like a mass of tadpoles, they had dropped suddenly into that bottomless pit and, disappearing from the surface of the earth, had dissolved into shadows. Whether Kō-san had waved the flag or not, whether he had attracted the attention of the others or not, now that I saw what had happened it made no difference. I would like to think of him vigorously waving the flag, but I was told that he had died in that hole and was lying with the other soldiers, chilled by death.

Stessel surrendered. There was peace. General Nogi made a triumphal return. The soldiers too were given a warm welcome home. But Kō-san had still not come out of his ditch. When I went unexpectedly to Shimbashi, and saw the tanned general, and the tanned sergeant with his little mother, I even shed a few tears and felt some joy in the event. At the same, I wondered why Kō-san could not climb out of the ditch. He had a mother too. She was not short, like the sergeant's mother, and nor did she wear straw sandals. If Kō-san had come back safe and sound from the battlefield and his mother had come to welcome him at Shimbashi station, she would certainly have clung on to his arm, just like the sergeant's mother. Kō-san would also have waited there on the platform, looking as if something was missing, for his mother to emerge from the crowd. As I thought about all this, I felt more sorry for Kō-san's mother, faced with the cruel reality of this world, than for Kō-san himself who would not climb up out of his hole. As soon as Kō-san had jumped into that ditch, when he made that dive, he had passed beyond worldly concerns. I could not worry about the time that he might have spent in this world; nothing would change for him, come rain or come sun, but it was not the same for his mother who was alone now and abandoned. See how it rains! She will keep to her room and all her thoughts will be with Kō-san. See how the weather improves! She will go out into the streets and will meet Kō-san's friends. On days when there are celebrations to welcome home soldiers returning from the front, and when we fly the national flag, she will be sad. "Ah, if only he were still alive!" she will complain. In the public baths, when a young woman of an age to marry draws a bucket of water for her, she will remember Kō-san, cherishing his memory, and sigh, "Ah, if only I had a daughter-in-law like her!"

Such a life can only bring her torment. If she had had many children, the presence of the others would have consoled her for the loss of one. But when there is only one parent and only one child, and the family is broken, like a pitcher split down the middle, the damage is irreparable There is nothing to hold on to. She is not the sergeant's mother; a person of her age has no one she can cling to. Hoping that Kō-san would return home, she had counted the days and nights on her wrinkled fingers and waited anxiously for the moment she would be able to embrace him again. But he whom she longed to embrace jumped unhesitatingly into a trench, waving the flag, and to this day he has not climbed out again.

Perhaps his white hairs had multiplied, but at least the general had come back to the cheers of the crowd. However much the sergeant's face had been bronzed by the sun, he had jumped on to the platform with an air of triumph. Even if he had some white hairs now, and his face was tanned, he had come back and his arm was there to be held on to. Even if his right arm had been bandaged or his left leg had been replaced by a wooden one, from the moment he returned to his country it would not have been important. But Kō-san had still not come out of his hole, and as he would never come out of it his mother would go after him and would throw herself into it to join him.

That day, by chance, I had a little free time and I was wondering if I should not go to Kō-san's house to offer some comfort to his mother, as I had not seen her for such a long time. It is right that I should go and console her, but whenever I visit her she cries and that troubles me. Last time I went to see her she sobbed for an hour and a half. After all her complaints had been exhausted, I found it very difficult to prolong the conversation. Then she said to me, "Oh, if only I had a calm daughter-in-law to give me courage!" And she began to develop her vision of this daughter-in-law so insistently that I found it very irritating. When this phase of lamentations was over, and I said it was no doubt best for me to leave, she told me, "There is something I absolutely must show you!" I asked her what it was. "It is Kōichi's diary!" she replied.

Indeed, the diary of a dead friend is something of interest. What we write in our diaries is not just a record of everyday events but a sincere expression of our emotions as we experience them. Consequently, we should never look at the journal of an intimate friend without his permission. In this case, however, the mother consented to it—in fact, rather, it was she who asked me to read it—and obviously it would be of great interest to me to see it. So when his mother suggested that I should read the diary, the prospect appealed to me and I was going to ask her to show it to me, but then I thought that I would find it very painful if the sight of this diary were to provoke fresh tears in her. With my customary inability, I would be unable to get myself out of the situation. Moreover, as my time was short and I had to meet someone soon, I said to her, "I shall come back soon to see you and I will ask you then to let me look at this diary with a clear head."

And upon that I escaped.

For the reason I have mentioned, I hesitated a little in paying her another visit. However, it was impossible to deny that I wanted to read that diary. If she burst into tears to a reasonable extent, I thought I could bear it. I am not made of wood or stone, and I am capable of showing compassion when faced with another person's misfortune, but I am not talkative by nature and get embarrassed when I have to express my feelings in words. In those circumstances, I don't know what to do. And when Kō-san's mother says through her sobs, "Will you listen to what I am going to tell you?" I never know how to react. Faced with such a situation, I try to preserve appearances and I must admit I am clumsy: my attempts at consolation are not only useless, but their consequences can sometimes be quite unexpected. This can go on until she has worked herself into a real turmoil, like water reaching boiling point. Under such circumstances, she must have trouble working out whether I have come to console her or anger her. So, if I do not visit her at all, I will not run any risk. If I do not take her any drugs she will not, as an indirect consequence, have the opportunity to poison herself. Let's postpone the visit until another time and drop it for today!

So I decided to defer my visit. But as I remembered what had happened the day before in Shimbashi, I could not help but worry a little about Kō-san. Unable to do anything else for him, I prayed for the repose of my old friend's soul. Writing verses of condolence is not in my line. If I were of a literary bent, I could have written about my daily relationship with Kō-san, as it really was, and get it published in a magazine—but I didn't know how to use my pen for that either. So what could I do? Well, I could go to the temple to pray! Kō-san has not yet climbed out of his trench in the Sung Shu-Sang fortress, but his hair, left so that he should be remembered after his death, has come from afar, has crossed the sea, and has been interred at the Jakko-in temple in the Komagome district. So I told myself that I must go to the temple, and I set off from my house in Nishikata-machi.[24]

It was just at the beginning of winter. The expression "little springtime," describing this time of year, always brings a feeling of pleasure with it, like the pleasure we feel at the prospect of a ripe *kaki*.[25] That particular year was exceptionally mild and I would go out with just a traditional jacket lined with wadding over my kimono. These clothes were light and easy to wear. Flourishing my stick, bent at the end with use, I contemplated an old painted sign displaying the characters "Jakko-in" in Prussian blue, in the style of Kōbo Daishi.[26]

---

[24] In December 1906, Sōseki Natsume moved house. He left the Komagome Sendagi-machi district, no. 57, for that of Nishikata-machi, no. 10; both were located in the Hongō suburb.

[25] The *kaki* is the fruit of the persimmon tree. It has a soft sweet orange pulp and looks like a tomato. It ripens during October and November.

[26] Kōbo Daishi (774–835) was a bonze who invented the Hiragana syllabary, and composed *iro-ha-ura* poetry, made up of the 47 syllables which comprise the Japanese language.

Temples are private places, and as I passed through the gate I experienced a familiar impression of solitude. I noticed how carefully the place had been cleaned, with not a single particle of dust to be seen, and felt gratified. Nothing is more pleasing to the eye than the sight of fine grain clay, not spongy or dried out but moist and the color of the sun. I don't know whether or not Nishikatamachi is a district where cultured people live, but it is certainly the case that there are no elegant houses there, or even a floor color that calms the mind. Many of the houses have been built recently. I have not yet looked at the matter scientifically and I can't say whether there is a lack of elegance because the number of intellectuals in the area has increased or just because the inhabitants' taste has become poorer. Nevertheless, when I entered the vast building, even I, who was normally quite content with a district fit for intellectuals, felt a desire to lead the life of a bonze. At the temple entrance, on both sides of the portal, were serene red pines, whose trunks were some ninety centimeters in diameter. They must have been growing in that place for a century. Such a noble prospect bestows confidence. I have been told that there was talk in the old days about the defoliation of pine needles during the tenth lunar month, but I have never seen a pine lose the smallest needle. Their roots were twisted around each other, portions of them, three to six centimeters in diameter and covered with knots, showing through the beautiful earth. Probably the old bonzes, the *bonzillons*—the priests responsible for the administration of the temple—or even the porters would sweep around them three times a day.

Beyond the pines on either side you could see, about fifty meters away, the main body of the temple. On the right was the accommodation for the bonzes. On the front of the temple hung a painted sign with gold calligraphy on it. The sacred character that the artist had wished to convey was marred here and there by what looked like bird droppings, or bits of *papier-mâché* that had been hurled at it. On the square, twenty-five centimeter thick Caucasus elm wood pillars hung Chinese sentences scribbled in the cursive style, which, because of this affectation, seemed to invite anyone who could to read them. I could not read them, and as it was impossible for me to decipher them, I was sure that they must be the work of great masters of calligraphy; more particularly, I thought of Wang Hsi Chich.[27] When I see ideograms which display their pretentiousness, and which I cannot decode, I want them to be the work of Wang Hsi Chich. If that master were not the author, I would not experience this sense of the old.

If you leave the central building of the temple to the right and turn left, you come to the cemetery. At the entrance there is an enchanted gingko.[28] I must point out here that "enchanted" is not my word. If what people say is true, everyone in the neighborhood knows of this tree in the Jakko-in temple as the "enchanted gingko." But however much they may insist that it is enchanted, it is difficult to believe because it is so large. It would take three men to encompass this giant tree with their arms. Each year the gingko sheds all its leaves and is left completely bare, looking like a shaven-headed bonze, and

---

[27] Wang Hsi Chich (307–335), a Chinese calligrapher.

[28] An ornamental tree from China with fan-shaped leaves, which grows to a height of about thirty meters. It is considered a sacred tree in the Far East.

uttering its plaintive cries to the violent autumn winds. But that year, because the temperature was so exceptionally mild, magnificent leaves still garnished its higher branches. If you stood at the foot of the tree and looked up, you saw the golden shapes bathed in a soft light and sparkling like tortoiseshells. It was a fascinating sight. Even though there was no wind, these golden shapes were rustling down around me. Of course, as the leaves were very thin they fell to the ground slowly and noiselessly. From the moment they detached themselves from the branches until they reached the ground, they reflected the light in different ways, depending on whether they were in sunlight or shade. They seemed to be in no hurry as they passed through these variations of light. Their fall was executed with infinite grace. As I watched them, it seemed that they were not falling but simply amusing themselves by fluttering about in space for a long time. A profound calm reigned. It is wrong to think that absolute tranquility demands a total absence of movement. It is when a single thing moves in a vast expanse of calm that we can perceive the tranquility that stretches beyond it. Furthermore, if this moving thing wavers long enough without exaggerating the degree of its movement, or if the movement in itself conveys an impression of calm, and the movement enables us to perceive tranquility elsewhere, we experience at that moment a feeling of profound calm. And this was precisely the effect that the gingko leaves created as they fell and fluttered through the air, undisturbed by a breath of wind. Because they were falling ceaselessly, morning and night, the fan-shaped little leaves covered the foot of the tree so completely that the black earth was no longer visible. I wondered whether the priests had not cleaned here because of the unpleasantness of the task or whether they had not swept up the piles of leaves because they liked them and wished to admire them. In any case, it was a magnificent sight.

I stayed for some moments under the gingko, sometimes gazing upwards and sometimes downwards. Then I left the tree and went into the cemetery. I had been told the place had a long history. I could see, here and there, stone graves on petal thrones, interwoven with lotus leaves. To the right there was one that was protected by a small barrier on which, in accordance with Buddhist custom, the posthumous name "Baikai seki den seki kaku" was engraved. This, doubtless, was the grave of a prince or of one of the intimate servants of the Shōgun. Among the inscriptions there were some very simple ones and others that were forty centimeters long. One of them showed the name "Jiundōji" engraved in a square—as it was for a child, the stone grave was small. There were many others. So many deceased names were engraved that the sight was sickening. However, all these inscriptions were old. It was not as if the number of people passing from life to death had dried up recently. In the past, the dead were received here as guests of this cemetery in the same inescapable manner year after year and would announce their presence on the little flaking tablets that carried their names. Once they passed under the enchanted gingko they immediately entered the world beyond, although it does not seem that the gingko had anything to do with that. But, now, so as not to restrict the places available in the cemetery, which were not after all very abundant, families coming to the Jakko-in temple to bury their dead probably accommodated their newly deceased in the family grave, which had welcomed ancestors from generation after generation. And Kō-san was one of the recently deceased who had been treated in this manner.

If we consider the antiquity of this cemetery, Kō-san's grave held an unquestionable authority in the community of graves. I don't know its exact age, but as it held his father, his grandfather and his great-grandfather, it was certainly far from recent. Apart from its age, it also occupied an advantageous location in the cemetery. Situated at the edge of the next temple, the Kawakami family grave, where Kō-san and his father and grandfather were resting, was raised above the others; it was located on a flat mound of earth, of about six or seven square meters. To get to it, you climbed up two stone steps and went right to the back of the cemetery. It was very easy to find: all you had to do was pass beneath the enchanted gingko, and walk in a straight line in a northerly direction for twenty meters or so. The route was familiar to me and I had already got halfway there when, all at once and for no reason, I raised my eyes and looked towards the place I was making for.

I could see that someone was already there. I didn't know who it was, because they had their back to me, but I could see that they were praying fervently, with their hands clasped together. I asked myself who it could be. In spite of the distance, I could tell by its appearance that it was a woman. Since it was a woman, it could only be his mother. Although I am indifferent by nature to women's fashions, and know nothing about them, I did know that Kō-san's mother generally wore a black satin belt over her kimono. When you see someone from behind, it is the belt that attracts your attention. Well, this woman's sash was not black at all. It was one of dazzling beauty that sparkled all over.

"It is a young woman!" I had spoken the words aloud without thinking. I felt embarrassed at the situation. I wondered whether I should go forward or turn back and I stood still for a moment. The woman did not notice anything and stayed huddled up, immersed in her fervent prayer in front of the Kawakami family grave. I was reluctant to approach her, that was the way of it, but at the same time I had done nothing wrong and had no reason to run away. I was still wondering about what to do when the woman stood up. Behind her, a thick high clump of bamboo showed flashes of green and it felt cold. The woman stood motionless in front of this thick bamboo with its great green drops of color. The background to this scene was in shadow; behind the woman there was an expanse of shade, due to the northern exposure, and her white face stood out against this dark background. She had large eyes, firm cheeks and a long neck. Her right hand hung at her side, and she held a handkerchief by the tips of her fingers. The snow-white handkerchief was a vivid spot of light against the dark bamboo. I saw nothing apart from the face and handkerchief of this woman, so illuminated by the purity of their whiteness. I experienced a moment of ecstasy.

I had seen many women—in the street, on the tram, in the park, at the concert, at temple feasts and fairs, but I was never as struck by any of them as I was by the sight of this woman. I had never before seen such a beautiful woman. I forgot Kō-san. I forgot that I had come to visit his grave. I even forgot my embarrassment. I was content just to look at the white face and the white handkerchief.

At first, the woman was completely unaware that there was someone behind her, but as soon as she began to move, apparently to leave the cemetery, I thought that she glanced distractedly in my direction and stopped for a moment on the stone steps. When our eyes met, at a distance of some ten meters, I was looking up at her from below and she had discerned me from above, and she promptly lowered her eyes to the ground. Then a dark crimson color suddenly spread across her features, although her cheeks remained white. I saw this crimson tint suffuse her whole face, and even extend to her earlobes. I felt very sorry for her and thought I would make off in the direction of the enchanted gingko. "But no! Because if I do that, she will think that I followed her surreptitiously. And it will be even worse if I gaze at her with dreamy fascination!" War strategists tell us that the way to get out of a desperate situation is to brave death and fight with all our might. The best thing, therefore, would be to advance with determination. There would be nothing surprising in this, because I had come to the cemetery to visit Kō-san's grave. If I carried on hesitating, I would arouse her suspicions. Having reached a decision, I gripped my stick firmly once again and walked quickly towards the woman. She too, still looking head down, began to move forward, and at the bottom of the steps she passed me furtively, as if she were fleeing, and brushed against my sleeve. A pleasant perfume wafted into the air and I thought I recognized heliotrope. The perfume was strong and I had the impression it was working its way through the back of my jacket, warmed by the Indian summer sunshine. After she had passed by, I felt reassured and restored to my usual state of mind. Then, wondering who it could have been, I turned round to look after her. At that moment, unfortunately, our eyes met again. This time, I was on the steps and I pressed my stick firmly on the ground. Turning sideways, she looked up at me. She was under the gingko, and the leaves of the tree were falling, fluttering and dancing, all the more elegantly because there was no wind, and touching her hair, her sleeves or her sash. It was one o'clock, perhaps half past. It was exactly at this time the previous winter that Kō-san, carrying the flag and exposed to the wind, had jumped into the trench targeted by the enemy guns. The sky had the limpid clarity of perfectly sharpened sabers lined up against a wall like a row of onions. The autumn sky, waiting for the coming of winter, seemed higher than at any other time in the year. The clouds, which could have been taken for gauze, drifted so slowly that we could scarcely see them move. If we had wings to fly up into the sky, our climb would have been endless. There was no doubt of that: that sky made me feel that the flight would never end. When we contemplate such a sky, we can sense the infinite very easily. The gingko unceremoniously divided the infinitely distant, infinitely vast and infinitely calm sky, and was changing into a golden cloud. Nearby, the tiles on the roof of the Jakko-in temple, like hundreds of thousands of fish scales, black and heavy against a fragment of the clear blue sky, reflected the warm rays of the sun. In the midst of this ancient sky, this secular gingko, the old Buddhist temple and the old graves that were distinguished by their calm and isolation, was this young and beautiful woman! The contrast was a sharp one. Against the background of the bamboo thicket, the whiteness of her face and handkerchief had arrested my gaze. Now it was the color of her kimono, which she had put on carefully and wore with ease, and her sash, which formed a ring in the very center of her clothes, that commanded my attention. I regretfully admit that I have no sense of taste and elegance and cannot describe the materials or specify whether they were striped or had some other pattern, but I am certain that the arrangement of the colors was magnificent. Clothes of this quality did not seem in place in a temple and its surroundings. I am sure such a place is far removed from their origin and purpose. I would have sworn that the pieces of fabric had been cut out in an exhibition gallery of the great Mitsukoshi[29] store and that they had been hung out for drying in the hermitage of the Rakushisa[30] mountain in Kyoto. They provided, I think, the greatest contrast with the surroundings. The young lady at the foot of the gingko had turned sideways to look at me, apparently to see which grave I had come to visit. Unfortunately, some suspicion about her arose in me and made me think back to the moment I had seen her on the steps. Suddenly, she took a path that led to the central building of the temple and resolutely made her way there. The leaves fluttering down from the gingko covered the black earth.

While I gazed at the woman as she went away, I thought again how singularly she contrasted with the surroundings. I had once seen a geisha in the Shintoist

---

[29] Mitsukoshi chinretsuba. The Mitsukoshi fabric stores set up exhibition galleries where customers would sit and browse through the fabrics to make their choice.

[30] Rakushisa, in the Sakyoku suburb of Kyoto, is famous for its association with the poet Matsuo Bashō, who lived there and dedicated a collection of poems to the place.

temple of Sumiyoshi[31], in Osaka. The beauty of her figure, with her "Shimada"[32] hairstyle in the autumn breeze, appeared to me even more ravishing than normal. In "The Valley of Hell" in Hakone,[33] amidst the geysers I encountered a Westerner, aged about sixteen, and thanks to that person the frightening and extraordinary scene of jets of boiling steam shooting up to ten meters high had soothed and consoled me. In general, our perception of contrast produces one of two consequences: either it reduces the intensity of a strong feeling or it impresses what we have been contemplating more deeply on us than before. This is what one would expect to happen, but it was not all the case on that day. The contrast I saw then did not weaken or deepen my former perceptions. It did not simply produce a heightened sense of antiquity, of isolation or of tranquility; the appearance of this woman in her magnificent clothing was more remarkable there than if I had met her at a concert or a garden party. The feeling which I had experienced on entering the Jakko-in garden was one of calm, of age and solitude. I even lost the sense of my own history, as if I had gone back to a time when my parents were not yet born. When I had looked at that woman

---

[31] Sumiyoshi or Suminoe is located between the cities of Osaka and Sakai. There is a Shintoist sanctuary there, famous for the legend attributed to it (it was founded by Jingū Kōgō, the mother of the Emperor Ojin, in the Kofun era, to thank the sea gods for allowing his military expedition to Korea) as well as for its architecture.

[32] A hairstyle of a woman of marriageable age. The tradition originates from the Kabuki theater.

[33] A district near Mount Fuji, renowned for its still active volcanic massif, its thermal waters and its springs, which are almost at boiling point. "The Valley of Hell" (Ōjigoku) is near the main crater.

standing in front of the bamboo clump, I had felt no sense of contradiction, and the moment that I had seen her figure turned towards me in the midst of the falling leaves I had the impression, on the contrary, that something more profound had been added to my previous thoughts. The old Buddhist temple, the tablet with the flaking Chinese characters, the enchanted gingko, as well as the still pines, the rows of graves mingled together, those old graves bearing the names of the dead, and a woman as beautiful as a flower—all these things merged together in my mind, and flowed into a single harmonious perception that filled me with unalloyed pleasure.

As you read these inept outpourings you may well be reluctant to accept the notions they express. Some will even dismiss them laughingly as intellectual twaddle. But the truth is the truth, even if it is perceived as a lie. Whether I am an intellectual or not, what I have written here is a true account of events, told without exaggeration, according to notes I made at the time. If you say it is bad to be a man of letters, I insist that I am not a man of letters. I am a researcher who lives in the district of Nishikatamachi. If you mistrust my ideas, I suggest that I explain this problem of contrast scientifically. My readers will certainly be familiar with Shakespeare's tragedy *Macbeth*. Macbeth and his wife conspire to kill their king, Duncan, while he sleeps. As soon as they have perpetrated their crime, someone is heard knocking repeatedly at the door. The porter appears on stage, saying "Here's a knocking indeed! Here's a knocking indeed!" and comes out with various wild and stupid drunken suggestions. Here is a contrast! And it is no ordinary one. It is like someone singing a comic song near a murder scene. What is curious is the fact that this comic episode does not in any way alleviate the atmosphere of desolation created by the previous scene. In the context of the play's development, the humorous interlude does not produce any comic perspective on the main action. But if we ask whether this interlude then has any effect at all, the reply is affirmative. It does indeed have an effect, and an extraordinary one. The atmosphere of desolation and dread that permeates the whole tragedy reaches the height of excitement through this character's facetious remarks. It could be said that his simple pleasantries manifest terror and that the buffoonery becomes an essential dramatic component that creates a climate of fear and makes the audience shiver. The explanation is as follows.

Without getting involved in lengthy discussion, it is clear that our personal point of view is ruled by our personal experience of the world and knowledge that we have acquired over the years. It is undeniable, I think, that the degree, variety and level of experience varies greatly from person to person. As for the wealthy man, born with a silver spoon in his mouth, with his constant experience of having his desires fulfilled with words such as "As sir wishes; it is an honor for me to fulfill sir's wishes," "sir" will perhaps end up thinking that people are born exclusively to bow their heads before him. Those fellows who have spent their money on alcohol, or women, or a beautiful house, and those who have bought themselves friends and have managed to procure themselves fifth rank in the Court,[34] giving them access to the Nobility,

---

[34] Jōgoi. The ranks go from one to eight. You are part of the nobility from the fifth.

well, these people will say that everything can be done
with money. So, keeping their hungry and loving eyes on
their safes, they will raise their noses towards the infinite
sky and ridicule the world of the poor. A single experience
will suffice. A rich gentleman who lost all his goods in the
great fire of Hakuyacho[35] will perhaps blanch whenever he
hears the Itabashi[36] alarm. A person who lost the roof of
his house during the great Nōbi earthquake,[37] but was
saved by a miracle, will probably invoke Buddha in his
prayers when he hears the boom of the cannon marking
noon.[38] An honest man, who has shoplifted just once in
his life will not be distrusted by his friends, while a man
who has led a life of deceit for ten years will find no trust-
ing friends if he is engaged in an honest pursuit for just
half a day. In short, our point of view on something is the
product of our experience over many years. As our lives
evolve in infinitely varied ways, these feelings that develop in us, whether they come from a business activity, our
profession, our age, the temperament nature has given
us or our sex, are different from one another. In the
same way, when we see a play or read a novel, and the

---

[35] *Hakuyaku-chō no Ōkaji.* This fire broke out on December 26, 1880 in
the Hakuya-chō district (Nihombashi suburb) and spread to thirty
other surrounding districts. Over 1,500 houses were destroyed.

[36] During the Edo era (1603–1868), Itabashi was a relay town, about
twenty kilometers from Edo (Tokyo) on the "Nakasendō" road, one of
the five traditional major trunk roads.

[37] This great earthquake occurred on October 28, 1891 in the region
between the towns of Mino (Aichi province) and Owari (Gifu
province).

[38] This midday gun salute was inaugurated in Tokyo in 1871 and ended
in 1929.

particular tone that pervades the whole work is reflected in our state of mind, this also unquestionably contributes to the sum of our experience. The more intense the experiences that lead us to a particular feeling, the stronger that feeling will be and the more fixed it will become. *Macbeth* is a tragedy that depicts in detail the actions, induced by experience, of old witches, of a shrew and a murderer. When we read the play from the start and reach the comic interlude with the porter, a unique feeling, caused by the experience of the play, creeps into our hearts, without our being aware of it, and that feeling is expressed by the word "terror." There has been terror in the past and the expectation is built up in the reader that there is terror to come. And it goes without saying that we can then interpret all the subsequent action of the play as in some way related to terror. That is what I want to say to you on this subject. Just as someone who has been seasick on a boat has the impression that the ground is moving when he returns to dry land, or as a sparrow, cowardly by nature, will distrust a fan believing it to be human, so will people who read *Macbeth* be left with a lingering sense of terror and not surprisingly will project it on to things that have no relationship with terror. And, since it occurs when that sense of terror is coloring our perceptions, the comic episode of the porter cannot be dismissed as simple banter, reminiscent of the comic interludes of the Noh theater.

We talk about "allusive" language—language that carries a double meaning: on one side of the coin is one meaning and on the other is its opposite. Everyone knows that we use the term "professor" as a synonym for an idiot and that "Shogun" is used as a nickname for a nobody.

This brings us to antitheses. Take a person for whom we used to have respect but who gradually becomes a fool in our eyes: we deride someone we used to praise. The more we apparently praise him, the more suggestive the implicit content of our words becomes. Is it not cruel to make fun of someone by arranging his shoes in a required order rather than giving him a simple low bow? I will try to examine this psychological phenomenon by developing my explanation a little. The logical propositions to which we normally have recourse are open to alternative interpretations. When we are uncertain as to what meaning to give to a particular expression, the perception that comes from our experience, to which I have previously referred, will come into play and we will easily find a solution to the problem of meaning. The same thing happens when we see or hear something comical. There is a serious meaning beneath the comic surface. Behind a hearty laugh hide bitter tears. The plaintive sobs of a ghost lie in the hidden meaning of a joke. So when a person who listens to the facetious language of the porter under the influence of the terror that has preceded it, will he take the scene at its comic face value or will he see something behind the comedy? If he looks beneath the surface, beneath the lie presented by the drunken porter, he will certainly perceive something that will make his hair stand on end. In contrast to explicit language, this allusive language conveys sarcasm with intensified ferocity. When we examine the nature of a beautiful woman who repulses even the simplest insect and see that beneath the nymph-like surface lurks a poisonous snake, her evil nature strikes us as far more frightening than it would if she were not so beautiful. It is the same with allusive language. A specter that visits us in broad daylight will inspire much greater fright than a ghost that follows the rules of the game and appears at night. It is the same with allusive language. If someone spends a night in contemplation in a ruined Buddhist temple and sees someone performing a comic dance under a cedar in the garden, shouting "Kappore! Amacha de Kappore!,"[39] that dance will fill him and his surroundings with horror. It is again the same with allusive language. The *Macbeth* porter is on exactly the same level as the comic dance in the temple. If we can understand the porter in *Macbeth*, we can certainly understand the effect of the beautiful woman in the Jakko-in temple.

Peonies, acknowledged as the queen of flowers, are so frail that when they fade and die even their rich and noble color cannot raise the slightest feeling of compassion in their admirers. A Japanese proverb holds that a beautiful woman has an unfortunate fate: "A plumed head is a big nuisance"—the durability of such a woman is not assured. However, these beautiful young women are usually full of vitality, and it is their hope in the future that illuminates them. The mere sight of them communicates a feeling of happiness. And they deck themselves in clothes of brightly colored patterns or satin, which demand our attention. Whenever we look at them, we are seduced by their elegance and magnificence. They are like nature in spring. And one of them, the prettiest of all of them, was in the Jakko-in cemetery. She stood there, framed by the somber, ancient and tranquil surroundings. It seems to me that

---

[39] A popular comic dance performed in the street whilst singing this tune. It dates from the end of the Edo era.

those ravishing eyes and splendiferous sleeves suddenly changed and became one with the deserted environment, and thus reinforced the sense of solitude and desolation that pervades the precincts of the temple. There is nothing more peaceful on earth than a grave, and yet when the young woman stood before the stele she seemed even more tranquil. The golden foliage of the gingko looked somber, an impression reinforced by its enchanted reputation. Yet, when this woman stood under the gingko, the profile of her face seemed even sadder, as if she were invoking the spirits from the tree. Why did this woman, dressed in clothes that would have been perfectly suitable if she had being going to Ueno[40] concerts or to a gala evening at the Hotel Imperial in Tokyo, convey an impression of solitude and desolation that imposed itself on the scene around her? Again, this too is like allusive language. Just as the *Macbeth* porter instills terror, this woman of the Jakko-in reinforced the impression of gloomy abandon.

When I looked at Kō-san's grave, I saw that someone had left wild chrysanthemums in a flower tube. They were white, like the wild chrysanthemums that flourish in hedges. This could only be the work of the woman I had just seen. I didn't know whether she had brought them from home in paper or whether she had bought them on her way there. I wondered why there was no card and even went so far as to look behind the leaves for one, but I could see nothing. Where could this woman have come

---

[40] *Ueno no ongakkai.* These concerts were held in the auditorium of the Tokyo Music School (now the Tokyo Arts University), located in Ueno Park.

from? Kō-san and I were close friends at high school and would often stay overnight at his house. I had met most of his family, but, counting on my fingers and trying to proceed in order, so-and-so, so-and-so, I could not remember having seen this woman. Perhaps she was not part of his family then? Kō-san was a sociable type and had a large circle of friends. But I had never heard that he had women friends. If he had had an intimate relationship with a woman, of course he would not necessarily have told me about it, but it was not in Kō-san's nature to hide anything like that from me. Even if he had kept it a secret from other people, he would surely not have kept it from me. It was odd to be thinking such thoughts. But I knew as much about the personal affairs of the Kawakami family as Kō-san, their direct descendant, did. This was for the good reason that Kō-san told me everything. Therefore, I was sure that if he really had had a relationship with a woman, he would have told me about it. As he had not done so, he did not know that woman. But then, there was no reason for an unknown woman to come and bring flowers to his grave. It was a mystery! Even if it were a rather strange thing to do, why shouldn't I just go off in search of the lady and ask her name, if nothing else? No, that would seem too strange. Why shouldn't I follow her covertly and find out where she lived? That would be acting like a private investigator and I did not want to associate myself with such a vile job.

"So, what could I do?" I asked myself, reflecting on the problem in front of the grave. Kō-san had jumped into the trench last November and he had never come out of it. However much I might strike my stick on the Kawakami family grave, however much I might shake it with my bare hands, Kō-san would continue to sleep at the bottom of his trench. He would continue to sleep without knowing that such a beautiful woman had come to his grave to bring him such beautiful flowers. This meant that he had no need to know her history or her name. And if Kō-san had no reason to know it, there was no need for me to pursue the matter. No, that would not do! That argument would lead to the conclusion that there was no need to look into the history of this woman and that would be a mistake! Why? After I have reflected on the reason a little further, I will give you an explanation. I felt sure of one thing: in the circumstances, I had to find out about her history. I would not feel easy unless I tried to find out about her by all the means at my disposal. So, abruptly and with a single stride, I jumped to the bottom of the stone steps, my feet scattering the leaves that had fallen from the ginkgo, and I went out through the gate of the Jakko-in temple. I looked to the left: she was not there. I turned towards the right: I did not see her there either. I rushed to the crossroads and scanned the horizon in all directions, as far as my eyes could see. She remained invisible. All things considered, I had let her escape. There was nothing to be done and I decided to talk to Kō-san's mother. Perhaps I would learn something from her.

3

The room of six tatamis faced south. At the edge of the veranda, which shone from polishing, there was a cedar wood towel rail. A washtub hung tastefully from the lower part of the canopy, suspended by a metal chain, and at the bottom of the veranda a clump of horsetails enhanced the charm of the place. On the other side of a bamboo fence stretched a field of tea bushes, covering about sixty square meters, and I could see three or four plum trees through the fence. Some traditional white socks had been washed and hung inside out on top of the bamboo fence to dry. Nearby was an upside-down watering can. At the end of the enclosure I saw a clump of flowering chrysanthemums so abundant that they looked like a composition in white jade, and I said to Kō-san's mother:

"How beautiful they are!"

"They are lasting a long time this year because of the mild weather. As you know, they were his favorite chrysanthemums."

"Oh! He liked the white ones?"

"Yes! He said that white chrysanthemums like those, with leaves like little white peas, were the ones he preferred. He was the one who brought the stalks here and planted them."

"Yes, I remember!" I said, inwardly feeling rather disturbed. The chrysanthemums that had been placed in the tube at the graveside at the Jakko-in temple belonged to that very same variety.

"Madam, have you been to the cemetery recently?"

"No, last time I caught a cold and had to stay in my room for five or six days. Completely against my will, I had to forego my visits to his grave. But even when I stay at home, my thoughts are always with him. You know, when you get older just going to the public baths is tiring."

"Going out walking in the streets is good medicine, I think. And these last few days it has been such good weather! So...."

"Thank you for your great kindness towards me. My close friends worry about me too and offer me advice. But anyway I don't feel well enough to go and there is no one who would willingly accompany an old lady like me."

When I get to a point like this in a conversation, I never know what to say. I had no idea what I could say to extricate myself from the situation, so, as I could do nothing else, I forced out the words "Aah, yeees! ...!" But the old lady seemed to want to grumble for a while. "Bother!" I said to myself, but as I could do nothing to change things, I watched a tit flying from one plum tree to another. The lady herself had interrupted the course of the conversation and she remained silent.

"If there were a young lady in your family, she could be company for you at such times."

For someone as much given to clumsiness as I am, I thought this a brilliant comment and was filled with self-admiration.

"Unfortunately, there is no such girl, and I tend to be reserved towards other people. Oh, if only my son had

had a wife, I would certainly be more comforted at such a time as this. What has happened is a great pity."

And so the daughter-in-law was on the agenda again! Every time I come to see her, she must always mention this daughter-in-law. It is normal for parents to want their son, when he reaches an age to marry, to have a wife, but to regret that a dead son has not left a wife seems to me to lack any coherent reasoning. I wonder whether it is just human nature—I don't know yet because I am not old enough to tell—but on the level of simple common sense it seems to me that Kō-san's mother is somewhat mistaken. Rather than have the prospect of being left alone and abandoned, people prefer to count on a suitable daughter-in-law to take good care of them. But let's put ourselves in the place of this daughter-in-law! Six months after the marriage, the husband goes to the front. After some time the war ends, and it is then discovered that the husband has died. In spite of being only twenty years old, the daughter-in-law is then obliged to spend her life in the company of her mother-in-law. Is there anything crueller than that? We cannot accuse Kō-san's mother of being unreasonable in her wishes, given her advanced age, but the desire shows great selfishness. Personally, I find that such behavior in elderly people displeases me enormously. However, if I make an ill-considered objection to her idea, I run the risk that she will take it very badly. Therefore, if I behaved so clumsily when I visited her with the express purpose of bringing her some consolation, I would be very ashamed. Understanding that the best thing to do is keep quiet and resolutely adopting that policy, I steered well clear of such comments. I am an honest man by nature, but as I live in society I try to not to arouse anyone's resentment and sometimes I am compelled to lie in this endeavor. As soon as honesty becomes compatible with daily social life, I will stop telling such lies.

"Yes, that's true, what happened is really a great pity. Why ever did Kō-san not find a wife?"

"Yes! We were looking at various possibilities when he had to leave for Port Arthur."

"So he was intending to get married?"

"Well!" was all she said, but then she remained silent.

This seemed a little strange to me. I wondered whether there were hidden clues connected with the Jakko-in temple matter. I confess to you that at that moment I was not thinking about Kō-san or his mother. My mind was filled with my desire to discover the identity of that singular woman and what relationship she could have had with Kō-san. That day I was not the sympathetic creature I usually was. I had transformed myself into what might be defined as "a placid person bursting with curiosity." Human nature changes from day to day. A wicked individual changes the next day into a good man. A worldly man during the day becomes a virtuous man at night. There are little masters who classify personality as if they can hold it in their hands. I call such people "intelligent fools." They cannot even study their own ego as it changes from day to day, and as they belch out their arrogant follies. I, too, I have not been afraid not only to think but also to declare publicly that the vile profession of private detective should not exist, and yet here I was dealing with a problem by quite clearly adopting the tactics of a detective—a phenomenon that fills me with astonishment. Kō-san's mother, who had hesitated for a moment to say anything, now began again in a resolute tone:

"Did Ko-ichi tell you something about it?"

"About a fiancée?"

"Yes! About someone he loved."

"No!" I replied. The question was exactly the one I wanted to ask her.

"Did Kō-san tell you about something?" I said.

"No!"

My last hope was crumbling away. As there was nothing to be done about it, I looked again at the garden. The tit had flown away and disappeared. The color of the chrysanthemums that I had noticed before provided a magnificent contrast with the damp black earth, which enhanced their whiteness. I suddenly remembered the diary that Kō-san's mother had mentioned before. It could well be that he had written something about this woman, of whom neither his mother nor I knew anything. And even if nothing was mentioned explicitly, if I read it thoroughly I might find something between the lines. As a woman herself, his mother would no doubt be incapable of discovering it. If I had a look at the diary, I would probably be able to detect something that would lead to a discovery. Nothing was now more important to me than to ask Kō-san's mother to allow me to read this document.

"The other day you told me about a diary, didn't you? Did he write anything in it about this?"

"In fact, until I read it, it didn't occur to me that there might be something in it, but I looked at it recently and then...." Suddenly, sobs interrupted her speech: I had again made her weep. How annoying that was! But, even if it annoyed me, it was now clear that there was something in the diary. And in that case, it didn't matter whether she cried or not.

"Is there something in that diary? I absolutely must have a look at it," I said very sharply. When I think about that today, I blush with shame. The lady rose and went into a back room.

A little later, the sliding door[41] opened and she came back with a pocket notebook in her hands. It had a brown leather cover and at first glance could be mistaken for a wallet. As Kō-san had taken this notebook everywhere, stuffed into one of his pockets, the brown cover had darkened and it had finger marks all over it. Without a word, I took the notebook from the lady's hands and was on the point of looking inside it when I heard the front door open with a bang and the voice of someone coming in. What an unwelcome visitor! With a wave of her hand, Kō-san's mother signaled to me to hide the notebook quickly. I slid it into one of the inside pockets of my jacket and asked her if she would let me take it back to my house to read it. She agreed, looking towards the front door. A serving woman informed her that Mr X had arrived. I had nothing to do with this Mr X! The only thing that had been important for me was to get hold of this diary, and now that I had it, I needed to get back home quickly and read it. Thinking this, I took my leave and made for the great highway of Hisakata-machi.

I passed in front of the Dentsu-in temple[42] and walked down the Omote-chō hill. As I went along I thought to myself that this was like a story in a novel, which made it seem unreal. And yet when I concentrated on the very real

---

[41] *Fusuma*, a mobile partition covered in thick paper.

[42] A Buddhist temple in the Koishikawa district where Sōseki lived.

events behind it, I dismissed this sense of unreality. It was, besides, extremely interesting. I absolutely had to investigate—no, that word "investigate" is disagreeable to my mind. I will say rather that I had to "do research": I absolutely had to do some research on the matter. In that regard, it was a shame that I had not followed the woman I had seen the day before. If I were unable to find her again, I thought to myself, I wouldn't be able to shed any light on the matter. Because of my pointless timidity I had let her slip between my fingers, even though she was not a shooting star that had passed from the light to the ocean depths,[43] and that was truly to be regretted. In fact, if we attach too much importance to dignity and display excessive refinement, such things frequently occur. If people do not have a little of the rogue somewhere in their personality they will never be successful. It is magnificent, of course, to be a perfect gentleman! But if a gentleman does not show some of the characteristics of a rogue, to a limited extent and without acting dishonorably, he will not be perceived by others as a true gentleman. We often say that he who is a gentleman in the strictest sense, and who does not have something of a roguish spirit in him, will die alone in the street. What if, from now on, I were to be a little more vulgar? I had abandoned myself to such stupid thoughts when I found that I had reached the Yanagicho Bridge. Just as I got there, an energetically pulled rickshaw, coming from the direction of Suidobashi, passed nimbly by and headed on towards Hakusan. It took only a

---

[43] Ryūsu kotei, "a shooting star that had passed from the light to the ocean depths," a quotation from a poem by Rai Sanyo (1780–1832).

few seconds for the vehicle to pass me, but by chance I
came out of my reverie and glanced up at the rickshaw.
The person inside disappeared from view in an instant,
but that face—who was it? By the time I realized it was the
woman I had seen in the Jakko-in temple, she had already
gone on a dozen meters. Here was the dreamt-for opportunity to be more vulgar. There she was! "Run after her!"
I told myself, as if that were nothing to me, and I started
off after her. But it was too crude to run off in pursuit of a
rickshaw—only a madman would do something so crazy.
Was there another rickshaw I could take myself? I looked
about in all directions but, alas, I saw none. Meanwhile,
the rickshaw with the woman inside was drawing further
and further away, and was now so distant that I could
scarcely make it out. I had failed again! I went back to
Nishikatamachi, plunged into a deep reverie. I wondered
if it were possible to succeed in anything on this earth
without becoming a scoundrel.

As soon as I got home, I shut myself in my study and
took the notebook out of my pocket, but the evening had
drawn in and it was too dark to make anything out without a light. In truth, I had already skimmed through the
notebook on my way back, glancing every so often at a
particular entry. But it had been written hastily in pencil
and it was not easy to decipher even in a good light. I
turned on the lamp. One of the servants announced that
dinner was ready, but I declined the offer and told her I
would take my dinner later. Now, starting with the page
and proceeding through the notebook in an orderly fash-
ion, I found that it dealt only with his experiences in the
army. I felt, too, that he had jotted down these notes
hurriedly, during the short moments he had been able to

steal for the purpose. Important things were described in one or two sentences: "It's windy. We ate two bowls of cooked rice in the underground tunnel. It's full of mud." "Since last night, I have felt the familiar symptoms of a cold coming on and I'm feverish. I didn't go to the doctor. I'm on duty as usual." "A lookout outside was hit by shrapnel. He fell against the tent and left bloodstains." "The signal for the main attack was given at 5 o'clock. A whole company was cut to pieces. It ended in a total fiasco. It's a tragedy!!!" Three exclamation marks appeared after "It's a tragedy." It seemed that these notes had been made to serve as a kind of memorandum. The notebook contained no well-crafted sentences. There was no trace of embellishment or careful composition in it. There was not even a minimal attempt to polish the style. And yet it was fascinating. His way of describing the actual events without embellishment pleased me greatly. I was especially pleased to see that he had not adopted the characteristically aggressive tone people often use when writing about war. Nowhere had he used vulgar and pretentious expressions like "Our hatred reaches to the sky! The Russians are full of arrogance! Let's cool the ardor of those hideous white barbarians!" His style pleased me greatly. "This is just what I would have expected from Kō-san!" I said to myself admiringly. But there was no mention yet of the important matter of the Jakkō-in. As I proceeded in my reading, I came across a page on which four lines of writing had been carefully crossed out. "That's suspicious!" I would not be satisfied until I had managed to make out what had been written there. I held the notebook very close to the lamp glass, pressing the document against it, and looked hard at it. Two-thirds of one character on the second line had escaped the crossing-out. It looked to me like the character YU. So, scrutinizing the passage as hard as I could, I managed to make out three characters that made up "Post Office." Underneath these three there were two others of which I could just distinguish a fragment: H*n*o. "What can that be?" I asked myself. For three minutes I studied this problem under the light of the lamp and then, finally, I understood. It was the Hongō[44] Post Office. Having made out this much with difficulty, I was unable to read anything else, whether I looked at the page backwards or upside down. In the end I gave up, but then, two or three pages further on, I happened on a great discovery: "As I had gone without sleep for two or three nights, I took a short nap in the trench. I dreamed of the woman I met at the Post Office."

I started involuntarily. "It's odd to dream of a woman I only saw for two or three minutes from time to time." From this sentence on, Kō-san had used a style that combined the spoken and written levels of language. "This must be a sign of how exhausted I am, but even if I had not been in such a state, I think I would have dreamed about this woman. Since I arrived at Port Arthur, I've seen her three times in my dreams."

I slammed the notebook on the table and exclaimed, "That's it! Here it is!" And now Kō-san's mother harping on about a daughter-in-law did not seem so nonsensical after all. She must have read this passage. That was the reason for it. Unaware of this, I had thought she was being

---

[44] A district in the suburb of Bunkyō-ku, where Tokyo University is situated, and where Sōseki Natsume worked for several months at the time he was writing this story.

selfish, I had accused her of cruelty—but I was wrong. Well, if she knew of such a woman, Kō-san's mother would have wanted them to be married, if only for one day—it was natural for a parent to want that. My lack of discernment had led me to misinterpret the feelings behind her constant complaint, "Oh, if only I had a daughter-in-law!" I had thought that it was just her desire to lessen her grief, but her words were, in fact, not selfish. She was alluding to the fact that her beloved son should have done what seemed right to him before he went to the front, even if it were only a fortnight before his departure. Truly, we are by nature uncaring, but as I was not then aware of these facts I could not have come to this con-clusion. Now, having recognized my former ignorance, another issue occurred to me. Was the woman mentioned by Kō-san indeed the woman I had seen in the Jakko-in? Or were they two quite different people? Was the woman he said he had met in the Hongo Post Office someone else entirely? I could not be certain from the evidence I had to hand, and so it was impossible to reach a neat conclusion. I would have to use my imagination if I were going to get anywhere. So, suppose Kō-san met a woman at the Post Office. We can reasonably assume that he did not go there for fun but very probably to buy stamps or to send or cash a postal order. It's possible that the woman stood next to Kō-san, and by chance saw the sender's name and address on his envelope as he was sticking a stamp on it, and memorized them. Putting a romantic gloss on this inci-dent, it was not beyond credibility that the woman at the Post Office and the woman at the Jakko-in were one and the same. In this light, it seemed that the mystery of the woman at the temple could be easily solved. But Kō-san's behavior was odd. Why did he have a recurring dream about a woman he had met only once? Hoping to find a more solid foundation for my theory, I continued reading and came upon the following passage: "A siege is one of the most difficult operations in modern military strategy, and it is no surprise that our troops suffer great losses, that many are killed or wounded, in carrying out such an operation. Over the last two or three months, so many officers have fallen at the foot of the fortress that it is impossible to list them all. Death will come to me too sooner or later. As I listen to the guns of the two armies day and night, I wait for my turn and wonder when my time will come." It seems that he had come to terms with this reality. On November 25 he wrote: "Tomorrow will be the day when I meet my fate." On this occasion, the text united the spoken and written levels of language: "It is normal for a soldier to die in battle. To die is an honor. From one point of view, to return alive to my country would be losing the opportunity to do my duty and die for it." On the day he was to fall on the field of battle, he had written: "Today will be the last day of my life. The rumbling of the guns that bombard the stronghold of Erh Lung-Shan with their destructive fire never stops. When I am dead, I will no longer hear that noise. And when my ears no longer hear, someone will come and visit my grave and will bring me a gift of little white chrysanthemum flowers. The Jakko-in temple is a peaceful place." Further on I read, "A violent wind is blowing. Now I am marching to my death. I shall advance waving our flag until a shell chances to pick me out. Mother must be cold." With these words the diary ended abruptly. It had to be like that.

I closed the notebook, shuddering. The story of this

woman worried me more and more, and it was becoming unbearable not to know her identity. As her rickshaw had been heading at top speed for Hakusan, she must surely live somewhere around there. If she lived in that district, it would be quite likely that she would go to the Hongo Post Office. But the Hakusan district is so large, that I had no chance of quickly finding someone whose name I didn't know just by wandering around it. Clearly this was not a simple problem that I could sort out that evening. As there was nothing else to be done, after dinner I resolved just to go to bed. In truth, I did try to read, but my thoughts were so distracted that the pages of my book might as well have been blank. So I decided there was nothing for it but to go to bed. As you can imagine, lying in bed did not work very well either and I passed a restless night.

The next day I went to the school and held my classes as usual, but what had happened preyed on my mind and I was unable to give my usual concentration to my lessons. Even in the staff room I had no interest in talking to my colleagues. I waited impatiently for the end of the classes and then walked to the Jakko-in temple to see what was happening there. There was no sign of the woman. I saw only the chrysanthemums that she had left there the day before; with their vivid brightness highlighted against the green bamboo, they looked like little snowballs. Then, leaving Hakusan, I walked around the districts of Haramachi and Hayasicho, but I saw nothing. I slept well that night because I was so tired, but when morning came I found again, just like the day before, that I could take no interest in my classes.

Two or three days after this, I asked a colleague

whether he knew a beautiful woman who lived in Haku-san. "Hmm! There are so many. You should move there!" he retorted.

As I was leaving the school, I caught up with a pupil and asked him if he lived in Hakusan. "No, I live in Morikawacho!" he replied.

I realized that all this stupid agitation I was feeling would not get me anywhere and I decided that the best thing to do was to regain my usual calm and devote whatever time was necessary to my investigations. With this in mind, I went into my study, which was as peaceful as ever, and, resisting any tendency to anxiety or impatience, I resumed a research project that I had recently begun.

The research in question concerned the serious subject of hereditary transmission. I am not a doctor or biologist by background, and so it goes without saying that I had no specialized knowledge on the subject of heredity—but it was precisely that lack of knowledge about the subject that had prompted my curiosity. My chance interest in the topic had led to a wish to learn both the history of research on heredity since its beginnings and all the new theories that had been developed in the field. This was the motive behind my research. It may seem simple enough to summarize in a few words the meaning of hereditary transmission, but the deeper one goes into it, the more complicated it becomes. A dedicated researcher could spend a whole lifetime on the subject. What I mean to say is that there are so many works by so many people that need to be read, such as Mendel's laws,[45] Weismann's theories,[46] the thesis developed by Haeckel,[47] his disciple Hertwig's research,[48] or Spencer's theories relating to evolutionary psychology.[49] That particular evening, in my study, my usual place for research, I intended to read a recently published book by an Englishman called Read.[50] I turned over two or three pages of it, without really paying attention and then, for some reason, the events recounted in Kō-san's diary imposed themselves on my thoughts and stopped me in my reading. Telling myself that I must not allow my study to be interrupted in this way, I began another page, but I was pursued by the image of the Jakko-in. I managed to chase it away and, then, just as I realized I had read five or six pages without difficulty, the image of Kō-san's mother's jacket and her well-groomed hairstyle was superimposed on my page. As I had determined that I would read this book, I had to make myself do it. I had to read it, but then a kind of theatrical interlude[51] inserted itself between my pages. Paying no attention to it, I continued to progress rapidly with my reading while the distinction between the theatrical interlude and

---

[45] Gregor Johan Mendel (1822–84), an Austrian botanist, discoverer of genetics.

[46] August Weismann (1834–1914), a German biologist and zoologist who worked on heredity and the evolution of the species.

[47] Ernst Heidrich Haeckel (1834–1919), a German zoologist, a follower of Darwin, who overturned the laws of evolution and descent.

[48] Oskar Hertwig (1849–1922), a German biologist and zoologist, renowned for his work on the fertilization of animals.

[49] Herbert Spencer (1820–1903), the English philosopher, one of the founders of nineteenth-century cultural and social evolutionism together with L. H. Morgan and E. B. Taylor.

[50] Carveth Read (1848–1931), an English philosopher who adopted a vision of the world based on panpsychism. His book *Natural and Social Morals*, published in 1909, was in Sōseki's library.

[51] Kyōgen, a comedy played between Noh intermissions, a comic interlude, a Kabuki play.

the contents of the book gradually diminished. Finally, the two became fused in my mind and I could no longer distinguish between the interlude and the text. For five or six minutes I was lost in this reverie and then, all at once, I came back to myself, as if I had had an electric shock. "But that's the answer! This matter can be resolved by reference to the phenomenon of heredity. By examining the problem in terms of heredity, I can find the answer!" I said aloud, giving voice to my thoughts. Until then I had jumped to the conclusion that this affair was very mysterious, that the story had a romantic undercurrent, that there was something unsettling about it, that I could not get my doubts out of mind and so that there was nothing else to do but to find this woman and question her. The result of all this was that my friends mocked me and I was going around Komagome like a rag-and-bone man. And yet I could not solve this matter by sheer force of will: even if I succeeded in finding and questioning the woman, I now realized with astonishment, it was not she who would shed light on the mystery. As anything she could tell would inevitably be strange to me, it would not put my doubts to rest. In the past, such phenomena of causality were known as Karma. It is an established fact that people resigned themselves to Karma, just as they might submit to the tears of a child and the stewards of the Shogun, as the proverb goes. Perhaps it was once enough just to explain everything away with the word Karma, but in the twentieth century our civilization cannot accept Karma as a rule to live by. Thus, rather than attributing a melodramatic or magical character to the story, I now decided that there was no other way to explain it than through the phenomenon of hereditary transmission. Normally, I would have to find this woman to determine whether she was, in fact, the same person Kō-san mentioned in his diary and, starting from that basis, would then carry out my research on the matter in the context of heredity. However, as it had proved impossible for me to find out this woman's address, there was no other way than to reverse the usual order of things and examine the lineage of Kō-san and this woman. That is, instead of going from bottom to top, it would be better to go from past to present. As the result would be the same, it mattered little.

So: how could I carry out my investigations into the ancestry of these two people? As I did not know who the woman was, I would concentrate first on the man. Kō-san was born in Tokyo, a native of the capital. I had heard that his father was born in Edo and that he died there, which would mean that he was a pure native of Edo.[52] His grand-father and his great-grandfather were also natives of Edo. It would seem, therefore, that Kō-san's family had lived in Tokyo for many generations. They were not trades people, craftsmen or vassals of the Shogun: according to what I had heard, Kō-san's family were vassals of the Prince of Kishu, and were transferred to Edo where they had lived for generations. The mere fact that it was a vassal family of Kishu provided me with useful information. The petty nobility of the clan, assembled around the Prince of Kishu, probably numbered several hundreds, but now, I thought, not many of them lived in Tokyo. Judging by the appearance of the woman, with her elegant clothes, her social position gave her access to the Prince's house—and

---

[52] *Edokko*, literally "a child of Edo." This term is used for the inhabitants of Edo.

if she had access to the Kishu clan chief, I would easily be able to discover her name. This was the hypothesis I was constructing. If it transpired that Kō-san and this woman did not belong to the same clan, I would still be in the dark with no hope of a solution. In those circumstances, I could do no more than wait for the chance of another meeting with her on the road that leads to the Jakko-in. However, if my supposition were correct, then everything else would flow from that, in accordance with my theory. According to my speculations, something must have occurred to bring an ancestor of Kō-san's into association with an ancestor of this woman—an occurrence which could clearly be interpreted as Karma. This was the second hypothesis I was constructing. As I developed the theory, it became more and more compelling. Now, I was not just satisfying my curiosity: the theory related directly to the research that I was conducting and the story thus constituted a case of great interest. As I developed this new approach to the problem, a feeling of well-being came over me. Until that moment, I had felt I was betraying my reputation and becoming squalid, like a dog or a detective. I had felt increasingly uncomfortable about the situation, but now, adopting this hypothesis as my point of departure, I could look on it as dignified and noble. It was a case of scientific research. I could look at things differently now, and I told myself there was no longer any reason to be racked by guilt about it. You can always find a justification for something by thinking about it in a different way. If you feel you are approaching a problem in the wrong way, you should simply sit down quietly and change the way you think about it.

The following day I spoke to a colleague at the school

who was from Wakayama[53] province. "Tell me, would you happen to know if there is some elderly person in your district who is well versed in the history of the Kishu clan?" I asked him.

"Certainly, I know someone," he replied, nodding his head.

When I questioned him further about this person, he gave me some rather interesting details. "He was formerly known as the head of the Prince's household. Now, he is called a 'steward,' but his duties haven't changed."

If he were a steward, so much the better: beyond any doubt he must know the names and positions of the people who frequented the Prince's house.

"Does this old gentleman have much historical knowledge? No?"

"Oh yes! He knows everything. It is said that he served the nation well at the time of the Meiji Restoration. He excelled in the use of the lance, you know."

That he was an expert in the use of the lance did not matter at all to me. What mattered was whether he could remember, coherently, any unusual reports and interesting anecdotes about the Kishu fief's dependants. I knew that if I just listened passively, my colleague would probably wander off the point.

"As he still carries out the duties of a steward, his memory must be accurate, mustn't it?" I said.

"If it were too accurate, that would be awkward: everyone in the Prince's house would be embarrassed. He is

---

[53] Wakayama province is the southern part of the Kii peninsula to the east of the city of Osaka. The town of Wakayama (400,000 inhabitants) is an hour by rail from Osaka.

nearly eighty and built like a rock. Such things are possible, you know. According to him, his good health is simply due to his use of the lance. That's why he gets up every morning at dawn and exercises with the lance, swirling it about in his hand."

"Enough about the lance. Could you introduce this old gentleman to me?"

"Whenever you wish!" he said, as a colleague who was nearby started to laugh and said to me, "You are really very busy, aren't you? You're looking for beautiful women in Hakusan and now you're on the look-out for grandfathers with good memories too!"

But I didn't think it was funny. If I could meet this old gentleman, I would easily ascertain whether I was on the right track or barking up the wrong tree. I needed to talk to him as soon as possible, and I asked my colleague if he would kindly write to the old man and let me know what date would be convenient for him.

Two or three days passed without any news, and then my colleague told me that he had just received a reply and that the old gentleman had invited me to come and talk to him the next day, at 3 o'clock in the afternoon. This made me very happy. That night, I let my imagination run riot as I considered various possible developments. First, I thought there was a 70 percent chance that I would uncover the truth as I hoped and that everything would become clear. These thoughts made me reflect that the strategy I had adopted in this matter (or, more truthfully, the lucky idea that had occurred to me) was really ingenious. An uneducated person would not have reflected on how such a theory could be applied. Indeed, even some educated people might be lacking in analytical ability and would consequently not have been able to develop the idea as I had done. With these thoughts going round and round in my head as I lay in bed, I was as proud as a peacock. When Darwin developed his theories on evolution or when Hamilton discovered the quaternion, they must both have felt like this. A bitter Kaki from your own garden tastes better than an apple you buy at the grocer's.

The following day, as my classes finished at noon, I waited impatiently for the time of the meeting. I went so far as to spend 25 sens[54] on a rickshaw to take me to Azabu, where I met the old gentleman. I will not reveal his name. To judge by his appearance, he was a man of bronze. He had a thin long white beard and wore a black kimono of Hachioji[55] fabric, with his family crest embroidered on it.

"Oh! So you are Mr ...'s friend," he said, mentioning my colleague's name.

I felt that he talked to me as if I were a child, as if he were superior to me—and here was I, about to make a great discovery and contribute to the development of scientific knowledge. Thinking about it now, I see that he did not really behave arrogantly. Rather, it was I who was being pretentious, and his greeting me as if I were just a normal person had seemed arrogant because of my own pride at the time.

After exchanging two or three common courtesies, we

---

[54] One *sen* was the hundredth part of a yen.

[55] A town of 460,000 inhabitants in Tokyo province. It is well known as a traditional center of textile manufacturing (Hachioji fabric, *hachiō- ji ori*, of which there are many varieties). Hachiōji was a former garrison town and today is a dormitory suburb of Tokyo.

got down to the issue in hand.

"Forgive me for asking what may seem a strange question, but did someone by the name of Kawakami once belong to your honorable clan?"

Despite my erudition, I was not familiar with the correct terms to use in social meetings of this kind. Using the term "clan" was normal, but I had said "your honorable clan" to show respect. Now I am no longer sure what to say in such situations: it seemed to me that the old man found it a little amusing.

"Kawakami? Yes, there have always been many Kawakamis. There was Kawakami Saizo, whose duty was to look after the Prince's house at Edo. His son Kogorō performed the same duties. He was the father of Koichi who was recently killed in the battle at Port Arthur. Perhaps you knew Koichi? What happened was very sad. His mother is still alive, I think?" He was drifting into a long monologue.

I had not made a special visit to a place as far away as Azabu just to hear all the details of the Kawakami family's business. I had mentioned the name of Kawakami because I wanted to know what relationship there had been between Saizo Kawakami and the woman in question. Unfortunately, as I didn't know the woman's name, I could not ask a direct question about her.

"Don't you have an interesting story to tell me about the Kawakamis?"

There was a curious expression on the old man's face as he gazed at me. Then he said seriously, "The Kawakamis? As I mentioned just now, there are several Kawakamis. Which one do you want to talk to me about?"

"I have no preference."

"You say that you would like to hear interesting stories. About what, for example?"

"Anything will do: I want to collect information."

"Information? What for?" What a persistent old man!

"There is a particular area I would like to investigate."

"All right! Kogorō was a patriot who was easily angered. At certain times, such as the restoration of the Emperor, he would let himself go. One day he came to me with a long saber strapped to his left side to argue with me."

"No! That's not what I'm looking for. Did nothing happen in their family that people still remember today?"

The old man thought about this in silence.

"What sort of man was Kogorō's father?" I asked.

"Saizo, you mean? He was extremely kind. He was the spitting image of Koichi whom you know. They were a lot alike."

"They were a lot alike!" I shouted, raising my voice sharply without realizing it.

"Yes, they were like two peas in a pod. I should tell you that during that period, some time before the Meiji Restoration, there was no social unrest. As Saizo's duty was to take care of our revered Prince's household, it is said that he led an elegant and refined life, and spent a lot of money."

"Was this man involved in a love affair? It may seem a strange question, but was there anything like that?"

"In fact, there is a sad story about Saizo. At that time there was a samurai called Tatewaki Onoda in our clan, who had an income of 200 sextaries of rice a year and who owned the house just opposite the Kawakami's place. This Tatewaki had an only daughter who was the most beautiful woman in our clan, you know."

"Go on, tell me about it," I said. This sounded promising.

"As the two families lived opposite each other, they spent a great deal of time in each other's company. The Kawakamis and the Onodas had a good relationship, and the young Onoda woman fell in love with Saizo. People said that she had become very emotional and had threatened to kill herself if she could not marry Saizo. Women are really hopeless! She begged her family with all her heart to let her marry Saizo."

"I see! So, did she marry him in the end, as she wanted?" This information was certainly convincing.

"Well, in fact, when Tatewaki sent someone to negotiate with Saizo's parents, it turned out that Saizo also wished to marry her, so the request ended in an engagement. The story goes that everything proceeded according to plan and even the date for the wedding was agreed."

"That's very good," I said, but in my mind I was thinking that if the wedding had indeed gone ahead that would be bad news for my theory, so I listened apprehensively to the continuation of the story. "Up to that point everything went well. And then an unforeseen obstacle arose."

"Ah well!" I said. I had been thinking that something must have happened to prevent the marriage.

"At that time, the Daimyo minister in Kishu had a son of about the same age as Saizo who was also sighing after Tatewaki's daughter. When the boy found out what was happening, he insisted that he should be the one to marry the girl. This was after she had been promised to Saizo. The efforts of the minister alone on behalf his son would have changed nothing, but his son had been the childhood companion of our revered Prince and they had grown up together. His Highness was therefore very attached to him. I don't know where or how the matter was effected, but our revered Prince communicated his wish to Tatewaki and asked him to give his daughter to the minister's son. Tatewaki had no choice but to accede to the Prince's request."

"That is so sad!" I said, but as my suppositions were all proving to be correct, one after the other, I could hardly contain my delight. Even in the case of something as tragic as the death of a dear friend, if we have predicted the event we experience a kind of satisfaction despite the sadness of the loss. If we remonstrate with someone and tell him he will catch cold if he doesn't wrap up, we feel somewhat annoyed if we find him well even though he has completely ignored our advice. We then fervently hope that he will catch a cold. As these examples demonstrate, people in general are selfish, so don't pick me out for special criticism!

"It was indeed a very sad business. As the instruction came from His Highness, the fact, for example, that promises had been exchanged was no argument and there was nothing to be done about it. So, in the end, Tatewaki made his daughter understand that she had to resign herself to her fate and broke off negotiations with Kawakami. As it was now untenable for the two families to live opposite one another, my father found himself entrusted with the job of arranging Takewaki's move into the Kishu fiefdom while Kawakami remained in his post at Edo. And I think it was to relieve his disappointment and frustration that Kawakami threw money down the drain at Edo. I can talk openly to you now about this matter because it is in the past, but at the time, as the honor of the families would have been severely damaged if rumors had been allowed to spread, the matter was kept relatively secret and most people knew nothing about it."

"Can you remember what this beautiful woman looked like?" This question was very important to me.

"I remember her very well. I too was young then, you know. When we are young, beautiful women take up most of our attention, don't they?" At this, he burst into laughter, covering his face with wrinkles.

"What was her face like?"

"Her face? I can't describe it to you in words. However, ancestry is something that no one can deny, and Onoda's youngest sister is her spitting image. You don't know Onoda—he is from the University too. He's a doctor in Arts and Crafts."

"Does he live near Hakusan?" I asked, scrutinizing his face for the answer and thinking that it must be so.

"You know him, do you? He lives in Haramachi. It seems the young woman is not yet married. She comes from time to time to the house to provide some company for the Princess."

Just as I thought! The matter was in the bag. That alone was more than enough for me. From start to finish, everything had proved to be as I had expected. It was the first time in my life that I had experienced such a feeling of contentment. There was no doubt about it. The woman of the Jakko-in was this young Onoda lady. I had never considered myself as a man of such penetrating powers of deduction. Here was a perfect example, with proof to support it, demonstrating the validity of my long-held views on the transmission of attraction. When Romeo saw Juliet for the first time he recognized immediately that she was destined for him, without a shadow of a doubt, taking account of the tens of years of experience accumulated by her ancestors. Helen believes that Lancelot is the love of her life when she meets him for the first time. This is surely because memories and feelings from an era long before her parents were born influence her thoughts. Twentieth-century men are prosaic: they mock men and women who fall in love at first sight, dismissing them as silly or frivolous romantics. But however ridiculous something may seem, we cannot twist the truth or turn it upside down. It is just believable that some may never have encountered this singular phenomenon, but if it happens before our eyes and we close our minds and continue to disbelieve it, that is simple stupidity. If one proceeded as I had done, fitting my investigations into a more general framework of knowledge and research, one should be able to produce an explanation consistent with twentieth-century concepts. By developing my ideas in this way, I felt that up to that moment I had done some brilliant thinking. But suddenly a thought occurred to me that puzzled me a little. According to the old man, he knew the young Onoda lady. He also knew that Kō-san had died on the battlefield. So these two young people who had enjoyed an amicable relationship with the same clan used to go to the Prince's house. Perhaps, then, they knew each other by sight? In that case, it is likely that they would have had an opportunity to talk to each other. Looked at in this light, the completely new theory of "heredity transmission" that I was professing did not appear so very convincing. If I could not confirm that they had met only once at the Hongo Post Office, my ideas would be in a fine mess. Still, since Kō-san had never mentioned to me any visits to the Tokugawas'[56] house, there was no danger I supposed. Moreover, as his diary had named the meeting place, there could be no mistake. However, to feel more secure about this possible flaw in my theory, I decided I would ask the old man about it.

"You mentioned the name Koichi just now. Did he often visit the house?"

"No! I only heard about him. As I have already told you, his father and I had an excellent relationship and we spent many evenings in engrossing conversation. I saw Kogorō's son when he was five or six years old. And I must tell you that, because of Kogorō's premature death, there was no subsequent opportunity for the family to come to the house. I never saw them again from that moment on."

That was the answer! It was as I thought. If this had not been the case, the story would have been incoherent, but this account formed an essential link for the demonstration of my theory. Now I was really reassured. Expressing all my gratitude to the old gentleman, I took leave of him. As I was leaving, probably thinking me the strangest visitor he had ever had in his life, the man remained at the front door after we had said goodbye. When I looked back after I had left the house he was still there, following my progress with his eyes.

I am going to cut the rest of the story short and tell it simply. I have already apologized to you for not being a man of letters. If I had been one, this would have been the

---

[56] Tokugawa, a Japanese aristocratic clan from the Minamoto dynasty that comprised the third, the last and the most important of the Shogun dynasties (1603–1867).

time to demonstrate my talents. However, my area of expertise lies exclusively in the reading of scientific works, and so I do not have the time to write lengthily about matters of the heart. At the welcome organized for our army at Shimbashi station, I felt deep emotion that brought into my thoughts the memory of Kō-san. Then, confronted with the mysterious occurrence at the Jakko-in temple, I analyzed the incident scientifically and produced an appropriate explanation. If this psychological journey has indeed been understood intuitively and rationally by my readers, the dominating theme of my story should end here. In fact, when I began to write the book, my joy at the prospect, and the energy it gave me, made me want to relate the events as precisely as possible. But, being unaccustomed to writing, I launched myself into a superabundance of detail. I included futile thoughts. And when I reread what I have written, I realized that my attention to detail is ridiculous. The fact that I have gone into so much detail up to this point now troubles me greatly: if I keep to the same approach, I will have to write another fifty or sixty pages to cover the remainder of the story. The examination period is approaching. I also have to get on with my research on the theory of hereditary transmission. Plainly, I do not have the time to indulge my brush on my sheet of paper. In addition, the essential thing that I wanted to achieve in this work was to bring the whole Jakko-in matter out into the open. As I have now done that, my mind is at rest and I can tell myself that it is enough. Suddenly I feel exhausted and I no longer have the energy to write more.

After my conversation with the old man, the logical thing for me to do was to meet Onoda, the doctor of Arts

and Crafts, a prospect which caused me no embarrassment. I obtained a letter of introduction from the same
colleague who had enabled me to meet the old gentleman.
Mr Onoda readily received me and talked to me. On my
second or third visit, a happy chance led me to meet his
sister. She was exactly what I had expected and was
indeed the person I had met at the Jakko-in. When we
met, although I thought that she would blush with embarrassment, she was open and straightforward and behaved
quite normally. This was contrary to my expectation and
struck me as rather odd. Up to then, everything connected with the matter had gone smoothly, but now something
troubled me: how was I to bring up the subject of Kō-san
in front of this young woman? As it was a delicate matter,
I could not, of course, just question her tactlessly about
him. All the same, if I didn't ask her about him, something
would be left unresolved. As far as I personally was concerned, I was now happy with the fact that my scientific
curiosity had been satisfied and it didn't seem constructive
to enter into what might seem an absurd and impolite
inquiry into the young lady's private life. But Kō-san's
mother, because she was a woman, wanted to know the
smallest detail. In Japan, unlike in the West, there has
been no progress in the attitudes towards relationships
between men and women. It was therefore unusual for a
single man such as I and an unmarried woman to sit down
and talk face-to-face. The fact was that if the opportunity
arose and I rashly brought the conversation round to this
subject, either I would needlessly embarrass the young
woman or I would find myself rebuffed: the young lady
would tell me that she did not know Kō-san. It would
be even more difficult to approach the subject in the

presence of her brother. In fact, it would not so much be difficult as boldly treading on forbidden ground. If the doctor knew that his sister was visiting Kō-san's grave, there would not be a problem—but if he did not know, I would be acting improperly by revealing a secret that was someone else's private business. If I behaved like that, however grandly I might display my knowledge of heredity, I would surely encounter an obstacle. I, so assured of my own intelligence and skipping about everywhere telling myself how talented I was, found myself confounded. Finally, I confided in Kō-san's mother. I told her the whole story, not omitting the slightest detail, and asked her advice.

Women are really very intelligent. She gave me precise instructions on what to say to Onoda:

"I know a lady who recently lost her son at Port Arthur and who spends her whole life from morning to night in sadness and solitude. I have tried to console her myself, but it is difficult for a man. I wonder whether your sister, when she has some free time, could possibly visit this woman occasionally?" I went straight to the doctor's house and repeated this like a parrot. Without any hesitation, Onoda gave his consent. Since that day, Kō-san's mother and the young lady have met from time to time. Each time they see each other there is a warmth between them. They go out for walks together. They lunch together. It is almost as if the young lady has become the old lady's daughter-in-law. The mother eventually showed the young lady Kō-san's diary. I wondered what her reaction would have been at that moment. She said: "That is why I went to the temple." And when she was asked why she had left an offering of white chrysanthemums on the grave, her reply was that white chrysanthemums were her favorite flowers.

I saw the general with the tanned face. I saw the sergeant an old woman was clinging on to. I heard the cheers of the people welcoming our soldiers. And I wept. Since Kō-san jumped into his trench, he has never come out again. No one has gone to welcome him home. Probably the only people who think about him on this earth are his mother and this young lady. Every time I see the intimate and cordial understanding that reigns between the two, my tears are purer and more refreshing than the tears I wept when I saw the general and the sergeant. The professor, apparently, does not know this story.

Titles by Sōseki Natsume

Inside My Glass Doors
Translated by Sammy I. Tsunematsu
ISBN 0-8048-3312-5

Originally published in daily serialization in the *Asahi* newspaper in 1915, *Inside My Glass Doors* is a collection of thirty-nine autobiographical essays penned a year before the author's death in 1916, written in the genre of *shōhin* ("little items").

The 210th Day
Translated by Sammy I. Tsunematsu
ISBN 0-8048-3320-6
The 210th Day, first published in 1906, is written almost entirely in dialog form. It focuses on two friends, Kei and Roku, and their behavior, as they attempt to climb the rumbling Mount Aso as it threatens to erupt.

Spring Miscellany and London Essays
Translated by Sammy I. Tsunematsu
ISBN 0-8048-3326-5

First published in serial form in 1909, *Spring Miscellany* is an eclectic pastiche—a literary miscellany—of twenty-five sketches, heir to the great *zuihitsu* tradition of discursive prose.

The Wayfarer
Translated by Beongcheon Yu
ISBN 4-8053-0204-6

Written in the years 1912–13, *The Wayfarer* explores the moral dilemma of individuals caught in the violent transition of Japan from feudal to modern society. The protagonist Ichiro is caught in a triangle with his wife Onao and his brother Jiro. What ensues is, in a sense, a battle of the sexes between a couple forced to live together by tradition.

Grass on the Wayside
Translated by Edwin McClellan
ISBN 4-8053-0258-5

Completed in 1915 during a period of rapidly declining health, *Grass on the Wayside* is Sōseki's only autobiographical novel and the first book of its kind to appear in modern Japan. It is the story of Kenzo, Sōseki's alter ego, an unhappy, self-centered man, one of the most fully developed characters in Japanese fiction.

The Three-Cornered World
Translated by Alan Turney
ISBN 4-8053-0201-1

In *The Three-Cornered World*, an artist leaves city life to wander in the mountains on a quest to stimulate his artistic endeavors. When he finds himself staying at an almost deserted inn, he becomes obsessed with the beautiful and strange daughter of the innkeeper, who is rumored to have abandoned her husband and fallen in love with a priest at a nearby temple.

Mon
Translated by Francis Mathy
ISBN 4-8053-0291-7

Mon is an intimate story of the consequences of an impulsive marriage, keenly portrayed in the daily life of a young couple and the quiet frustration, isolation and helplessness they face as they live a lonely and frugal life alienated from friends and relatives.

Kokoro
Translated by Edwin McClellan
ISBN 4-8053-0161-9

Written in 1914, *Kokoro* provides a timeless psychological analysis of a man's alienation from society. It tells the story of a solitary and intensely torn scholar during the Meiji era and his chance encounter on the beaches of Kamakura with a young student, who gradually learns the reasons for the scholar's aloofness and withdrawal from the world.

My Individualism and The Philosophical Foundations of Literature
Translated by Sammy I. Tsunematsu
ISBN 0-8048-3603-5

These essays, which originated as lectures, explore issues close to Sōseki's heart: the philosophical and cultural significance of isolation, belonging and identity associated with rapid technological, industrial and cultural change. Sōseki defines the role of art and the artist in light of the loneliness and individualism of the modern world, and attempts to create a Japanese theory of literature.

❤❤❤TUTTLE CLASSICS❤❤❤

LITERATURE

ABE, Kobo 安部公房
The Box Man 箱男 4-8053-0395-6
The Face of Another 他人の顔 4-8053-0120-1
Inter Ice Age 4 第四間氷期 4-8053-0268-2
Secret Rendezvous 密会 4-8053-0472-3
The Woman in the Dunes 砂の女 4-8053-0207-0

AKUTAGAWA, Ryunosuke 芥川龍之介
Japanese Short Stories 芥川龍之介短編集 4-8053-0464-2
Kappa 河童 0-8048-3251-X
Rashomon and Other Stories 羅生門 0-8048-1457-0

ATODA, Takashi 阿刀田高
The Square Persimmon and Other Stories 四角い柿 0-8048-1644-1

DAZAI, Osamu 太宰治
Crackling Mountain and Other Stories 太宰治短編集 0-8048-3342-7
No Longer Human 人間失格 4-8053-0756-0
The Setting Sun 斜陽 4-8053-0672-6

EDOGAWA, Rampo 江戸川乱歩
Japanese Tales of Mystery & Imagination 乱歩短編集 0-8048-0319-6

ENDO, Shusaku 遠藤周作
Deep River 深い河 0-8048-2013-9
The Final Martyrs 最後の殉教者 4-8053-0625-4
Foreign Studies 留学 0-8048-1626-3
The Golden Country 黄金の国 0-8048-3337-0
A Life of Jesus イエスの生涯 4-8053-0668-8
Scandal スキャンダル 0-8048-1558-5
Stained Glass Elegies 短編集 4-8053-0624-6
The Sea and Poison 海と毒薬 4-8053-0330-1
Volcano 火山 4-8053-0664-5
When I Whistle 口笛を吹くとき 4-8053-0627-0
Wonderful Fool おバカさん 4-8053-0376-X

TUTTLE CLASSICS

NAGAI, Kafu　永井荷風
A Strange Tale from East of the River and Other Stories　墨東綺譚
　　4-8053-0266-6

NATSUME, Soseki　夏目漱石
And Then　それから　0-8048-1537-2
Botchan　坊ちゃん　0-8048-1620-4
Grass on the Wayside　道草　4-8053-0258-5
Kokoro　こころ　4-8053-0746-3
I am a Cat　吾輩は猫である　0-8048-3265-X
Inside My Grass Doors　硝子戸の中　0-8048-3312-5
The Miner　坑夫　0-8048-1577-1
Mon　門　4-8053-0291-7
Spring Miscellany　永日小品　0-8048-3326-5
Ten Nights of Dream, Hearing Things, The Heredity of Taste
　　夢十夜、他　0-8048-3329-X (4-8053-0658-0; Japan only)
The Three-Cornered World　草枕　4-8053-0201-1
To The Spring Equinox and Beyond　彼岸過迄　0-8048-3328-1
　　(4-8053-0741-2; Japan only)
The 210th Day　二百十日　0-8048-3320-6
The Wayfarer　行人　4-8053-0204-6

NIWA, Fumio　丹羽文雄
The Buddha Tree　菩提樹　0-8048-3254-4

OE, Kenzaburo　大江健三郎
A Personal Matter　個人的な体験　4-8053-0641-6

OOKA, Shohei　大岡昇平
Fires on the Plain　野火　0-8048-1379-5

OSARAGI, Jiro　大佛次郎
The Journey　旅路　0-8048-3255-2

SAWAMURA, Sadako　沢村貞子
My Asakusa　私の浅草　0-8048-2135-6
SHIGA, Naoya　志賀直哉
The Paper Door and Other Stories 襖、他　0-8048-1893-2
SUMII, Sue　住井すゑ
The River With No Bridge　橋のない川　0-8048-3327-3

TUTTLE CLASSICS

TAKEYAMA, Michio　竹山道雄
Harp of Burma　ビルマの竪琴　0-8048-0232-7

TANIZAKI, Junichiro　谷崎潤一郎
Diary of a Mad Old Man　瘋癲老人日記　4-8053-0675-0
The Key　鍵　4-8053-0632-7
The Makioka Sisters　細雪　4-8053-0670-X
Naomi　痴人の愛　0-8048-1520-8
The Secret History of the Lord of Musashi and Arrowroot
　武州公秘話、吉野葛　4-8053-0657-2
Seven Japanese Tales　谷崎潤一郎短編集　4-8053-0640-8
Some Prefer Nettles　蓼喰う虫　4-8053-0633-5

TATEMATSU, Wahei　立松和平
Distant Thunder　遠雷　0-8048-2120-8

UCHIDA, Yasuo　内田康夫
The Togakushi Legend Murders　戸隠伝説殺人事件　0-8048-3554-3

UNO, Chiyo　宇野千代
Confessions of Love　色ざんげ　4-8053-0613-0
The Sound of the Wind　宇野千代　人と作品　4-8053-0614-9
The Story of a Single Woman　生きてゆく私　0-8048-1901-7

YOSHIKAWA, Eiji　吉川英治
The Heike Story　新平家物語　0-8048-3318-4

ANTHOLOGY

Donald Keene
Anthology of Japanese Literature　日本文学選集　4-8053-0662-9
Modern Japanese Literature　現代日本文学　4-8053-0752-8

Ivan Moris
Modern Japanese Stories:An Anthology 近代日本文学 0-8048-1226-8
　(4-8053-0751-X; Japan only)

Lane Dunlop (tran.)
A Late Chrysanthemum　晩菊、他　0-8048-1578-X

TUTTLE CLASSICS

CLASSICS

IHARA, Saikaku 井原西鶴
Comrade Loves of the Samurai　男色大鏡　0-8048-1024-9
Five Women Who Loved Love　好色五人女　0-8048-0184-3
The Life of an Amorous Man　好色一代男　0-8048-1069-9

JIPPENSHA, Ikku 十返舎一九
Shank's Mare　東海道中膝栗毛　0-8048-1580-1

L. Zolbrod (tran.)
The Tale of Ise　伊勢物語　0-8048-3338-9
　(4-8053-0740-4; Japan only)

YOSHIDA, Kenko 吉田兼好
Essays in Idleness　徒然草　4-8053-0631-9

Mother of Michitsuna 道綱の母
The Gossamer Years　蜻蛉日記　0-8048-1123-7

MURASAKI Shikibu 紫式部
The Tale of Genji:2 Volumes (Seidensticker)　源氏物語
　4-8053-0676-9
The Tale of Genji (Suematsu)　源氏物語　0-8048-3256-0
The Tale of Genji:2 Volumes (Waley)　源氏物語　4-8053-0660-2

A.L. Sadler (tran.)
The Ten Foot Square and Tales of Heike　方丈記、平家物語
　0-8048-0879-1

Howard Hibbett (tran.)
The Floating World in Japanese Fiction　浮世草紙の世界
　0-8048-3464-4

HISTORY

Edwin O. Reischauer
Japan : The Story of a Nation (4rd Ed.)
　日本：その歴史と文化（第四版）　4-8053-0666-1

G.B. Sansom
A History of Japan (3-volume Set)　4-8053-0375-1
Japan : A Short Cultural History　4-8053-0317-4

TUTTLE CLASSICS

Helen Craig McCullough
The Taiheiki : A Chronicle of Medieval Japan　太平記　0-8048-3538-1

J.W. Hall
Japan : From Prehistory to Modern Times　4-8053-0661-0

R.H.P Mason and J.G. Caiger
A History of Japan　0-8048-2097-X

W. G. Aston (tran.)
Nihongi　日本書紀　0-8048-0984-4

OTHERS

Inazo Nitobe
Bushido　武士道　0-8048-3413-X

A. B. Mitford (Lord Redesdale)
Tales of Old Japan　日本の昔話　0-8048-3321-4

Elizabeth Gray Vining
Windows for the Crown Prince　皇太子の窓　0-8048-1604-2

Ruth Benedict
The Chrysanthemum and the Sword　菊と刀　4-8053-0671-8

Henry Scott Stokes
The Life and Death of Mishima　三島由紀夫―死と真実
  4-8053-0651-3

John Nathan
Mishima : a Biography　三島由紀夫伝　4-8053-0639-4

Stephen F. Kaufman (tran.)
Musashi's Book of Five Rings　五輪の書　0-8048-3520-9

John Allyn
The 47 Ronin Story　0-8048-0196-7

William Dale Jennings
The Ronin　0-8048-3414-8